Moving behind her, Irish leaned in. "Why are you trying so hard to resist me if you think it's a lost cause?"

Mallory shivered. He wanted to press his lips to that spot, but it wasn't time yet. She had to make the first move.

"It's messy," she said.

"It doesn't have to be."

"Says the man whose life isn't lived surrounded by very observant family members."

"I can be very sneaky when motivated." He leaned closer to her neck, so his breath would be hot against her skin. "And I'm very motivated."

"Dammit." The word seemed torn from deep down inside her as she turned to face him, and then she gathered the front of his shirt in her fist and hauled him toward her.

Irish wasn't much of a romantic, but as his mouth finally claimed Mallory's, he thought of fireworks exploding against a night sky.

He cupped the back of her neck. Her skin was so soft, and so were her lips. This woman was soft and sweet, and he needed to be gentle.

But then his sweet, gentle woman made a low growling sound in her throat and threaded her fingers through his hair, and he forgot to hold back. He put his other hand on her waist as his tongue slid between her lips.

Dear Reader,

Welcome back to Sutton's Place! Mallory, the middle Sutton sister, doesn't expect to open her door and find a cowboy camping in her yard. Neither did I at first, which makes the title *An Unexpected Cowboy* even more fun. Most of my heroes are from New England and have easy smiles and strong family connections, but Irish showed up from Montana in his hat and boots, and his stoic kindness stole my heart.

Mallory has her hands full with the brewery, her family and being a single mother, but there's something about Irish she won't be able to resist for long. Especially once he decides he's going to stick around for a while, which is definitely unexpected!

You can find out what I'm up to and keep up with book news on my website, www.shannonstacey.com, where you'll find the latest information, as well as a link to sign up for my newsletter. And you can also reach me by emailing shannon@shannonstacey.com or look me up on Facebook at Facebook.com/shannonstacey.authorpage.

I hope you enjoy Irish and Mallory's story and hanging out with the friends and family of Sutton's Place Brewery & Tavern. Happy reading!

Shannon

An Unexpected Cowboy

SHANNON STACEY

Recycling programs for this product may not exist in your area.

ISBN-13: 978-1-335-40850-1

An Unexpected Cowboy

For questions and comments about the quality of this book, please contact us at CustomerService@Harlequin.com.

Harlequin Enterprises ULC
22 Adelaide St. West, 41st Floor
Toronto, Ontario M5H 4E3, Canada
www.Harlequin.com

Printed in U.S.A.

A *New York Times* and *USA TODAY* bestselling author of over forty romances, **Shannon Stacey** grew up military and lived many places before landing in a small New Hampshire town where she has resided with her husband and two sons for over twenty years. Her favorite activities are reading and writing with her dogs at her side. She also loves coffee, Boston sports and watching too much TV. You can learn more about her books at www.shannonstacey.com.

Books by Shannon Stacey

Harlequin Special Edition

Sutton's Place

Her Hometown Man

Blackberry Bay

More than Neighbors
Their Christmas Baby Contract
The Home They Built

Carina Press

Boston Fire

Heat Exchange
Controlled Burn
Fully Ignited
Hot Response
Under Control
Flare Up

Visit the Author Profile page
at Harlequin.com for more titles.

Chapter One

We received word from an observant reader this morning that a camper has appeared next to the Sutton's Place Brewery & Tavern. Is somebody planning a vacation? Has a sibling squabble led to temporary exile from the house? Or perhaps the Sutton family has a guest visiting from out of town and there's no more room at the (former) inn. Only time (and the *Gazette*) will tell!

—*Stonefield Gazette* Facebook Page

"Mom, I can't find my backpack! I think it's in the car."

Thank goodness it was Friday because Mallory Sutton was so over this week. The boys had the last week in April off from school, but she had to get through two more weeks of these daily battles first. She went to the bottom of the stairs to yell back to Eli, even though she hated bellowing through the house. Sometimes it was the fastest way to get things done. "If you left your backpack in the car, how did you do your homework?"

"Didn't have any."

Eli was only in the third grade, so there was a good chance he wasn't fibbing. Fifth-grade Jack was the one she really had to keep her thumb on. They'd started the school year with a phone call from Jack's teacher because his essay about his summer had bragged about how he hung out in a bar, brewing beer. Luckily, Mrs. Avery lived in Stonefield and knew the Sutton family had converted the carriage house on the property into Sutton's Place Brewery & Tavern, and they'd laughed about it together.

Since her mom was about to put breakfast on the table, Mallory grabbed her keys and went to hunt for Eli's backpack in her car. They were usually walkers, but it had been raining yesterday, so she'd picked them up and she was sure he'd had it. She found it on the floor of the back seat, and she was thankful the boys liked hot lunch from school because if he'd left a lunch box in there, her car would probably stink.

It wasn't until she stood up straight, slinging his backpack over her shoulder, that she saw it.

Next to the huge carriage house—deep green with cream shutters and trim to complement the Queen Anne main house—which her family had turned into a brewery to fulfill her late father's deepest wish was a camper. And not a tiny camper, but one of those big fifth-wheel types, and parked near it was the biggest pickup truck she'd ever seen. With full-size doors for the back seat and a full-length bed, it looked as long as a school bus.

As she stared at the camper, which hadn't been there when she went to bed, the door opened and a man stepped out. A tall, muscular man in battered cowboy boots, well-worn jeans and a dark blue long-sleeve, button-down shirt, was settling a cowboy hat as battered as his boots onto his head as he stepped down.

Mallory didn't exactly flee, but she wasted no time going back into the house and closing the door behind her. Then she threw the dead bolt, and leaned against the door to calm herself. A very attractive man was camping in her yard, and she had no idea what she was supposed to do about that.

Her mom came around the corner into the living room. "Breakfast is ready, so… What's the matter?"

"There's a cowboy in the yard."

"I'm sorry, there's a *what* in our yard?"

"A cowboy. And a camper." She forced herself to

stop and take a deep breath, moving away from the door. She could see by the look on her mother's face that she wasn't making sense. "I went outside and there's a camper parked on the back side of the tavern. And a cowboy came out of the camper. Boots. Hat. Like, an *actual* cowboy, I think."

"Why would a cowboy park his camper in our yard? Maybe he's lost and doesn't know he's in the wrong place."

"Mom, there's no way he missed the big sign that says Sutton's Place Brewery & Tavern. What are the chances he mistook that for a campground? Maybe Lane hired a bouncer. He looks like he would be a really good bouncer."

"What on earth would we need a bouncer for? We've known most of our customers for our entire lives."

They both turned toward the door when a heavy knock sounded on the wood, and Ellen stepped forward. "I'll get that."

"Mom, I can't let *you* open the door. I'll do it."

"Maybe we should call Case and have him bring Boomer over."

Mallory considered the suggestion for a few seconds. Case Danforth had lived across the street since they were kids, and now her older sister, Gwen, had moved in with him. He wouldn't waste any time crossing the street if they called him for help. Their shepherd-and-lab mix, Boomer, might look and sound scary if he wanted to, but he'd probably be best friends with the cowboy in two minutes or less.

And it was very unlikely a serial killer would set up a camper in the yard. Not impossible, but it definitely wasn't the most logical conclusion.

"This is ridiculous," she said, walking toward the door and yanking it open.

Maybe a mistake, she thought as she took in the full effect of the man on the porch. Up close, he looked taller and his shoulders broader. He wasn't a lean guy, but it looked like the weight he carried was all muscle. She'd have to run her hands over his body to be sure, of course, but that would be incredibly rude and possibly also dangerous, so she curled her hands into fists.

And those eyes. The man had icy pale blue eyes framed by the dark hat and beard, and when their gazes locked, a shiver went through her.

"Hi," was all she managed to say, as though she didn't have a whole lot of questions to ask him, ranging from who he was to why he appeared to be camping in their yard.

"Lane didn't tell you I was here, did he?" he asked in a voice that, of course, had to match the body. Low and rough, and she absolutely wasn't going to imagine that voice saying naughty things in her ear later.

"Oh," Ellen said, jerking Mallory out of thoughts she had no business thinking. "I have a voice mail from Lane on my phone, but I haven't listened to it yet. They're usually about the brewery."

"I have one, too," Mallory admitted. "I was ignoring it until the boys leave for school."

She pulled out her phone and pulled up Lane's voice mail message, putting it on speaker.

"Hey, Mal. There's a camper next to the brewery and it belongs to a friend of mine. His name's Irish, and he's from Montana. He got in late last night and I was going to have him follow me to my place, but I have to move some equipment around before that camper will fit, so it was easier to park it there for the night. The house was dark, so I didn't bother knocking. He's a good guy and I'll be over later."

"Montana," Ellen said as Mallory slid her phone back into her pocket. "That's a long drive."

"Yes, ma'am."

"You must be hungry. I was just getting ready to put breakfast on the table," Ellen said, gesturing for him to come inside. "Nothing fancy, but come eat."

He looked as if he was going to decline the invitation, which would suit Mallory just fine. She didn't have time for tall, dark strangers with a look in his pretty blue eyes that made her realize just how long it had been since she'd been this attracted to a man. She had kids to send off to school.

But it had been more of a command than an invitation, so he stepped forward. As Mallory moved out of the way so he couldn't accidentally brush his body against hers and cause her to spontaneously combust, he removed his hat and ran his hand through his thick, dark hair to smooth it and she almost burst into flames anyway.

She really needed to get hold of herself.

"I'm Ellen Sutton," her mother said, holding out her hand after closing the door.

"It's nice to meet you, Mrs. Sutton," he said, shaking her hand. "I'm Irish."

"Please, call me Ellen."

"Okay…ma'am."

Mallory noticed the way he hesitated and got out of using her first name. "I'm her daughter Mallory."

Even though she tried to brace herself for the contact, the touch fully roused every need and desire she'd been tamping down for a long time. His hand was hard and calloused and much larger than hers, but his grip was gentle.

It also lingered for a few seconds longer than his handshake with her mother, his blue eyes looking at her as if he was trying to figure something out. He didn't seem to talk much, but maybe her view on that was skewed because nobody in her family ever *stopped* talking.

"Is Irish your first name or your last name?" Ellen asked.

He didn't simply let go of Mallory's hand. Instead, he drew his away slowly, his fingertips skimming over her palm before he turned to her mother. "It's just Irish, Mrs.…ma'am."

She smiled and waved a hand at him. "If it's actually hard for you to call me Ellen, you *can* call me Mrs. Sutton. Either way is fine for me."

His relief was so visible, Mallory almost laughed out loud. But footsteps running down the stairs—how many times in their lives had she told her sons not to run on the stairs—reminded her they were on a schedule here and already behind even before an unexpected cowboy turned her morning upside down.

Irish had no idea what was happening, or how he'd ended up in this kitchen, eating scrambled eggs with a family he didn't know.

The boys—Jack, who was ten, and nine-year-old Eli, according to Mrs. Sutton—were the spitting images of their mom. Dark blond hair and blue eyes, with a whole lot of energy. They were doing their best not to stare at him, but they were too curious about the strange man in the kitchen to hide it. He couldn't really blame them. He hadn't expected to be sitting at their table with them this morning, either.

The other thing he hadn't expected was taking one look at Mallory Sutton and having hunger—to touch her and kiss her and run his hands over those curves—hit him like a cattle prod.

But he was going to ignore that jolt of attraction because he was here to visit a friend and check out the brewery. He was *not* here to get tangled up in anything messy and Lane had mentioned in passing once that Mallory didn't have a husband. If Irish knew one thing about relationships, no matter how casual or short, it was that getting involved with a single mom was always messy.

"So what do you do, Irish?" Mrs. Sutton asked once they were seated around the kitchen table. They'd passed a dining room on the way in, but it looked like the huge table in there was currently being used for a jigsaw puzzle.

"I've worked ranches my whole life, but now I'm traveling and seeing some new country." He hoped that answer would satisfy her because he didn't really want to go into more detail.

"Ranch is my favorite!" Eli yelled, almost knocking his brother's juice glass off the table.

"I only like ketchup," Jack said.

Irish had heard somebody say a person could learn anything by watching a YouTube video, and he wondered if there was one that would teach him how to understand what kids were talking about.

"He's not talking about salad dressing, boys," Mallory said, reaching out to move Jack's juice glass toward the center of the table. "The cowboy kind of ranch."

"Are you retired, then?" Mrs. Sutton asked. "Or are you just taking a long vacation?"

He should have guessed she wasn't done with the

questions. "I'm not sure, ma'am. I was the foreman for a big spread for a number of years, but the ranch recently passed to the owner's son, and he and I had some differences of opinion on how to do things. I've never seen the ocean, so I figured I'd head east and stop by and see Lane on the way."

Mallory was looking at him when he said it, and he guessed some of that anger over the employment situation was showing on his face because she arched an eyebrow before changing the subject. "So I gather you're the cowboy Lane met when he went to school in Montana."

"Why did Uncle Lane go to school in Montana?" the younger boy asked. "Is Montana far away? Did he have to ride the bus?"

"College, honey," Mallory said. "Uncle Lane got his degree in forestry in Montana, which is pretty far away."

"Did you have to get gas on the way here?" Jack asked, and Irish wasn't sure what that had to do with anything, but he nodded anyway.

Mrs. Sutton chuckled. "That's how he measures distance. If you have a full tank of gas and you go somewhere, but have to fill up before you get back to town, it was a long drive."

"My truck takes diesel," he told Jack, "but I definitely had to fill the tank a few times."

"A truck that big pulling a camper like that?" Mrs. Sutton snorted. "Probably more than a few times."

"Lane said you were interested in brewing, too," Mallory said, and he was thankful to be saved from the possibility they'd try to calculate his gas mileage. "Have you done any?"

"Some home brew stuff," he said, dipping his head slightly to the side. "Never had the time or the space to do more than that."

"I'm surprised Lane hasn't shown up yet," Ellen said. "He should be here to show you around."

"Last night he told me there was a job he couldn't get out of this morning, but he'll be here as soon as he can."

He knew Lane owned a tree service with his cousin Case—it had been started by their fathers and they inherited it—and that the cousin was marrying Mallory's older sister. And Lane used to be married to Mallory's younger sister, Evie.

Not having any family himself, he had a little trouble wrapping his head around the many connections he was walking into. He'd heard a lot about the Sutton family from Lane, of course, but remembering it all and matching it to faces while navigating breakfast with strangers wasn't a well-honed skill of his.

But he remembered the bigger picture. Lane Thompson and David Sutton had dreamed of opening a brewery together and they'd finally made the leap—both of them putting themselves up against a financial wall in order to renovate the Suttons' carriage house—and then David had passed away the January before last. Mallory had finally made her sisters, Gwen and Evie, come back to Stonefield to help and together they'd managed to get it all done. Gwen had also fallen in love with Case, who lived across the street, during that time and was staying, but Lane expected Evie to up and leave town anytime.

"You're going to be late, boys," Mallory said. "Let's go."

As the boys ran out of the kitchen, Irish stood and gathered his dirty dishes. "Thank you for breakfast, Mrs. Sutton. It was delicious."

She waved his words away, but she looked pleased. "You're welcome anytime. I'll take those."

"I can wash up," he said. It seemed only fair, since she'd done the cooking.

"Case installed a dishwasher for me last month and now there's nothing to it. And I'm sure you have a lot to do to get settled."

"If you could tell me the best place to buy some groceries, I'd appreciate it. I'm running low on some things. And once Lane gets here, I'll hook up and get that camper out of your way."

"Nonsense," Mrs. Sutton said. "It's not in the way. And if you take it to the Thompsons', the only place it'll fit is where they park the tree service equipment and that lot is ugly and dusty. Plus, I don't know if you noticed, but back when this place was an inn, they installed all the hookups for a camper off the carriage house because the owners had one. David kept all that up because he thought we might buy one someday when the kids were gone. I have no idea how he thought we were going to open a brewery *and* run around in an RV at the same time, but that was David. Dream big and the details will work themselves out."

Irish took a second to sort through all the words coming at him—the Sutton women talked a lot, and they did it fast—but the bottom line seemed to be that she was inviting him to stay on the property while he was in New Hampshire.

He looked to Mallory for her reaction, since she had small kids and should have a say in who was around the house, but she gave her mom an affectionate eye roll and then smiled at him.

That smile made him ache deep inside.

"There's no sense in arguing with her," Mallory told him. "She usually gets her way, and she's right. Our yard is a lot nicer than Lane's equipment lot, plus the brewery's right there."

He shouldn't. There was something about the way he felt every time Mallory Sutton looked at him that should have him hooking his truck back up and hauling that fifth-wheel up the road without looking back.

"Sounds good, if you're sure," was what came out of his mouth.

"I'm sure," Mrs. Sutton said firmly. "And you'll want to go to Dearborn's Market for groceries. We need a few things, so Mallory can go with you and show you the way."

He saw the woman in question pause in the act of ushering her kids—who'd yelled a goodbye as they ran past with their backpacks, making him wonder if they ever slowed down—out the door to school. Maybe they were just that friendly around here, but there was a hint of a maternal matchmaking vibe to the offer that surprised him. He'd never seen himself as the kind of guy a mother would want for her daughter. He tried to come up with a way to get Mallory out of the obligation, but his mind had gone fairly blank other than imagining how nice it would be to have her riding in his truck with him, a country song on the radio and the wind blowing her hair.

He really needed to get a grip.

Before he could come up with a reasonable excuse to turn down Mrs. Sutton's offer of her daughter's company, Mallory rejoined the conversation. "Your vehicle or mine?"

Irish couldn't remember the last time he was a passenger. He always drove. "I've got coolers in the back of my truck already."

"I'm off to work," Ellen said after locking the dishwasher and hitting a button. "Mallory, check the list on the fridge and if I think of anything else I need, I'll let you know. Have fun exploring Stonefield, Irish."

“Thank you, ma’am,” he said dutifully, though grocery shopping and exploring the town were two different things. He was planning to buy some food, not do a scenic walking tour before visiting the gift shop, though with Mallory for a tour guide he might not mind so much.

“I have a few things to do before we go,” Mallory said.

“So do I,” he said. If he was going to be staying here for a few days, he needed to level the camper properly and hook it up. “But I’ll be ready whenever works for you.”

After she nodded, he walked out of the house and paused on the front porch before settling his hat on his head and heading for the camper.

He had no idea what he’d gotten into here, but between the rambunctious boys, their bossy grandmother and their extremely attractive mom, he suspected it was going to be a wild ride.

Chapter Two

Next week is Spring Cleanup Week at the dump, when you can get rid of unwanted items without paying a fee! The public works department has asked us to remind you that they don't accept hazardous materials, paint cans or dead bodies.

—*Stonefield Gazette* Facebook Page

Once she was buckled into Irish's passenger seat and had the chance to check out her surroundings while he walked around to get in—because of course the man who couldn't even call her mother by her first name had opened and closed her door for her—Mallory decided the cab of his truck was bigger than the entirety of her small SUV. It certainly felt that way, anyway.

And when he turned the key in the ignition and she heard the low rumble of the diesel engine, she frowned, noting how close they were to the house. She should have heard the truck last night. "Maybe we should install one of those doorbell cameras that alerts your phone if there's movement outside."

"I'm sorry."

She turned her head to find him looking at her, his expression like stone. Did the man ever smile? "Sorry for what?"

"For making you feel unsafe in your home."

It took her a few seconds to realize she'd spoken her thoughts about a doorbell camera aloud, and that he was blaming himself. Which wasn't totally untrue, but not the whole story. "I don't feel unsafe. It's more that maybe we need to rethink the certainty one of us would wake up if something was happening over here by the carriage house. When you started your truck, it made me realize it's a little loud and it had to have been running for a while to get the camper parked where it is, but nobody in the house woke up."

"I'm pretty good with backing up gooseneck trailers of any kind, so it didn't take long." He put the truck in gear and pulled out onto the road in the direction Mallory pointed.

"But still," she continued, "you showed up. Lane

showed up. There were truck doors opening and closing. This truck running. A camper being unhooked. It's not so much feeling unsafe as just being aware, with money and alcohol on the property, we might need a better security system than hoping we wake up."

"Your future brother-in-law and his dog were over, too."

She snorted. "A whole welcome-to-Stonefield party we slept through."

"If it makes you feel better, Case said your sister—Gwen, right?—slept through it, too. I guess your family's just heavy sleepers." He took a left turn when Mallory pointed. "And you and Mrs. Sutton both slept through phone calls from Lane, so I'm not sure your doorbell texting your phone would do much good."

She laughed, assuming he was teasing her, but when she glanced at him, there was no smile from him. He was relaxed behind the wheel, so it wasn't tension. Apparently he just suffered from Resting Stoic Face. "Good point, although my mother never knows where her phone is and mine was charging in the kitchen."

They'd reached what passed for downtown Stonefield, so she told him he should grab a parking space wherever he found one, since the tiny market parking lot was almost full, and he nodded once to let her know he'd heard her. But when they passed Sutton's Seconds—her mother's thrift shop—for the second time, she thought of all the times Case and Lane had grumbled about the sizes of parking spaces in town. And they had normal-sized pickups.

"Who designed the parking in this town?" Irish asked, his voice a low growl that made her shiver.

"Probably people who didn't foresee anybody grocery shopping in a yacht-sized truck." She pointed. "Wait, pull in that lot. We can park there."

He did as he was told, parking the truck across several spaces, but he didn't turn the engine off. "Cyrs Funeral Home? We can't park here."

"Sure, we can." She pulled up the ongoing text thread she had with Molly, whose parents owned the funeral home, to send her a message. "I'm telling Molly whose truck it is and why it's here."

"What if it's in the way?"

She shook her head. "There are no funerals today."

"How do you know?"

Text sent, she turned to look at him, her lips curved in amusement. "Well, nobody's died, so it would be weird for the Cyrs to be putting on a funeral."

He still hadn't turned the engine off, and he was drumming his fingers on the top of the steering wheel. "It feels wrong."

"Look, Molly's been my best friend since kindergarten, so I get that some people are weirded out by funeral homes, but you get used to it."

"I'm not weirded out," he said, turning that icy blue gaze on her. "It feels disrespectful."

"If there was a funeral planned for today, it would be." She didn't want to sit in this giant truck and argue all day with a man she'd just met. "Just think of it as Molly's house instead of a funeral home. Or you can keep driving around town until you find half a damn street worth of parking spaces all empty at the same time."

He finally killed the engine and the sudden silence was a relief. And of course, by the time she'd unlatched her seat belt and tucked her cell phone back in her purse, Irish was there to open her door.

He also held out his hand to help her down. Though she was perfectly capable of climbing out of the truck, thanks to the running boards down the side, she decided to take the opportunity to touch him again. In her mind, her feet hit the ground and instead of releasing her, he pulled her hard against his body and told her he'd been dreaming of kissing her since he knocked on her door that morning.

In reality, as soon as her feet hit the pavement, he let go of her hand and waited for her to move so he could close the door.

But the daydream had been nice while it lasted. "If you get a lot of stuff, we can wheel the cart over here as long as we bring it back. Their lot's so small, they're used to it."

"I don't need a lot. Mostly milk and some meat to put on the grill."

She assumed his camper had one of those little grills that hung on the outside. "You're welcome to use our grill if you want. And I should probably warn you that my mother's going to insist you eat with us. As far as she's concerned, you're our guest."

"Guests are invited," he said as they crossed the street. He walked with a long, confident stride and she had to hurry to keep up. He must have noticed because once they were on the sidewalk again, he slowed.

"You were invited," she felt compelled to say. "Lane told you to stop by if you were ever in New England. We just didn't know when you were coming."

"It's not Lane's house."

She laughed. "Like that matters. He's been like family for our entire lives—and actually was for a little while—and he owns half the business. Plus, none of that is important. You're in Ellen Sutton's world now."

They reached the market and she was amused when he stood to the side and gestured for her to enter, as though he was holding a door that automatically opened and closed. He might not say much or smile at all, but somebody had drummed good manners into him. Or maybe it was a cowboy thing.

She knew being in Dearborn's Market with a man nobody had ever met—and not just a man, but a man like Irish—was going to be the talk of the town before they'd even walked out the door. Even without the hat and boots, he commanded attention. And they were certainly getting that. Mallory was pretty sure that Donna wasn't reading her phone at a weird angle while stocking shelves, but was sneaking a picture of her and Irish together.

He wasn't a browser, instead focusing in on whatever was on his mental list—mostly dairy, eggs and half the meat aisle—and the only thing on the Sutton's fridge list was brown sugar. Her mother sure had latched on to that flimsy excuse to send her off alone with Irish fast, though.

In what felt like record time to Mallory, they'd wheeled his groceries back to the funeral home. She was about to tell him she'd hand stuff up to him if he wanted to get in the bed of the truck, but he dropped the tailgate and pulled out two massive coolers, setting them on the ground.

By the time he'd divvied up the groceries between the two and added the ice he'd bought, she was itching to point out he should have brought the groceries to the coolers and not the other way around because they were going to be too heavy to lift back into the truck.

Then he swung the first cooler up onto the tailgate as though it was a single bag of groceries and her mouth went dry. Definitely all muscle, then.

Thank goodness he was only staying for a few days.

"Mal!"

She turned to see Lane walking toward them, and she hoped he hadn't noticed her ogling his friend's cooler-lifting body as he got near. Lane wasn't a hugger, so he smiled at her and then, after the second cooler was loaded and the tailgate closed, shook Irish's hand.

"I stopped by the thrift shop to apologize to Ellen for her waking up to a stranger parked in her yard, and she told me you two were around town somewhere. Want to grab an early lunch before we head back to the brewery?"

Mallory was going to decline the invitation because being in Irish's orbit was intense and she wouldn't mind some alone time to give herself a stern talking-to about what a bad idea it would be to throw herself at a man who'd just shown up in her yard that morning.

But Irish gave one short nod of his head. "I could eat."

Okay. But she could still beg off and head to the thrift shop. She figured Irish could find his way back to the house, but if he wasn't sure about it, he could follow Lane. She was about to excuse herself when Lane patted the back pocket of his jeans, where she knew he kept the small notebook she and her sisters had given him for his birthday last week.

It was a pocket version of the leather-bound journal their father had written notes about brewing in for years, and which Lane had referred to often while they were opening the brewery. Evie had found a place that would emboss the brewery's logo into the leather and, while the notebook inside could be changed out, the cover would hopefully last forever. It was gorgeous and had even helped Lane overcome his natural aversion to writing things down.

"I have a few questions for you, Mal, so we can go over them while we eat."

So she was doing this. "Sure. Let me run the cart back."

"I can do that," Irish said, because of course he would, but she shook her head and started walking with it before he could grab it.

She gave herself that stern talking-to while she walked to the cart corral, which was ridiculously close to the door instead of out in the parking lot. Being attracted to a man who was just passing through made no sense. And she doubted his legal name was *just Irish, ma'am.* She knew nothing about him, really. The lecture continued on the walk back, and even while they all walked together to the diner. It did nothing to dampen her awareness of the man at her side.

"Lane, did you get approval for the autumn brew yet?" she asked, flailing for any topic that could distract her, and Lane obliged her by launching into a rant about the constant bureaucratic red tape he had to navigate. Not her favorite kind of distraction, but at least it was a temporary fix for her runaway imagination.

* * *

Stonefield had the kind of diner made up of a long coffee counter and booths in the main dining room, though Irish saw some tables in a side room that Lane and Mallory didn't even glance at. Hat in his hand, he followed them to an open booth, and he expected Mallory to slide in first, on the same side as Lane.

But the two of them were talking and, as if out of habit, Mallory sat across from Lane. Irish didn't want to squeeze in next to Lane, so when he stepped up to the end of the table, he knew he'd be sitting next to Mallory. And they weren't big booths.

She looked up at him and he saw the realization in her eyes. "Oh, I can just..."

She started to slide toward the end, but she'd have to get up and Lane would have to get up to let her in on the inside because his legs were longer, and that didn't make any sense. "This is fine."

After a second of hesitation, she smiled and slid to the inside, giving him room to sit. After hanging his hat on his left knee, Irish cleared his throat and took the menu Lane handed him from the metal rack that also held a sugar dispenser, ketchup and the salt and pepper.

As he scanned the offerings, the conversation around them slowly returned to normal. Since they'd been talking to each other, he doubted Lane and Mallory had noticed, but a hush had fallen over the place when he walked through the door. Whether it was because he was a stranger in town or because they'd never seen a man in a Stetson before, he couldn't say.

"Everything's good here, by the way," Mallory told him. "And the special's fish chowder."

Irish couldn't stop the full body shudder at the thought, but it was worth it because it made Mallory laugh at him. He liked the sound a lot, and didn't mind being the object of her amusement. "Not really a seafood guy. Or a chowder guy."

They all ordered burgers, and he wasn't surprised most of the lunch talk revolved around the brewery. From what he could tell, the business had been everybody's primary focus since Mallory's father died, and it had only been open for six months. There were probably still a lot of kinks to be worked out.

The entire time they ate and conversed, Irish was keenly aware of how much space he took up. The booth wasn't very big, and trying to keep his body from touching Mallory's took some effort on his part. But despite his best efforts, their arms occasionally touched for fleeting moments. Shifting his leg had caused it to brush against hers. Innocent, unavoidable touches that would normally go unnoticed if his entire body wasn't already far too aware of her proximity for his comfort.

Lane insisted on paying the bill, which didn't sit

well with Irish, but his friend was stubborn and said he could pay next time.

Next time.

He wasn't sure he'd be in town long enough for a next time since he was only staying for a few days, but he wasn't going to argue about it. After standing and settling his hat on his head while Mallory slid to the outside of the booth, he put out his hand to help her up.

She looked confused for a few seconds and then gave him a smile that was part thanks and part teasing as she reached for him. The teasing didn't bother him. He didn't remember much about his mother, but he remembered her drilling manners into him and he used them even if people thought he was old-fashioned.

Then her hand was in his, and how could a touch go on too long and yet be too fleeting at the same time? When her fingers slid up his palm, a part of his brain wanted to drop his hand—to not feel that warm contact. But a much larger and more vocal corner of his brain urged him to keep holding her hand once she was on her feet. And he did for a few seconds, waiting for her to withdraw her hand.

She didn't. The diner's buzz faded into the background as her gaze met his and he felt as if he was falling into her dark eyes. There was nothing but his heartbeat and her skin against his until she slowly—and seemingly reluctantly—pulled her hand from his.

"Thank you, sir," she said in a voice that made him think of hot nights and tangled sheets.

"Anytime, ma'am." He watched the quick rise of her chest and the slight parting of her lips as she took a breath, and there was just a hint of a blush across her cheeks.

Yeah, she definitely felt it, too.

Lane did all the talking on the walk back to where they'd parked, giving Irish a rundown on the brewing operation, but he'd have to tell him again later because Irish's mind was on the woman who was beside him. Since Lane was on the tall side, too, Irish had deliberately slowed his pace so Lane would do the same and Mallory wouldn't have to practically jog to keep up.

He liked having her beside him, even if she was quiet because Lane didn't leave many openings in the conversation when it came to talking about beer.

Since they were all going to the same place, he figured Mallory would ride with Lane. On the one hand, he kind of liked having her in the passenger seat. He could steal glances at her and listen to her voice as she pointed out where things were in the town. But on the other hand, maybe it was best he use the drive back to give himself a hard lecture. He was just passing through and maybe he wouldn't mind the temporary company of a pretty woman while he was in town, but it wouldn't be fair to her. And it was no way to repay the family's hospitality. He needed to keep his hands—and his mind—off of Mallory Sutton.

"I should walk over to the shop," she said, and the pang of disappointment let Irish know that, whether it was logical or not, he'd *really* wanted her to ride back with him and that was disturbing. His resolve he wasn't going to return the Sutton family's hospitality by thinking wayward thoughts about Mallory had lasted about two and a half seconds. "Mom said something about meeting Laura after work, so I can bring her car home."

"*My* mom mentioned a short meeting at the library," Lane said, and Irish remembered that his mother answered the phone and handled other things for the tree service since she'd been doing it for her husband and brother-in-law before they passed away and didn't see any reason to stop doing it. "She can run Ellen home after."

Just like that it was settled and after a breezy goodbye wave, Mallory started walking away. Irish considered himself a man with exceptional willpower, but not watching her leave tested even his limits. It didn't matter. His mind had already memorized the way her curvy butt and hips swayed in jeans, so he didn't need to look and could keep his attention on Lane.

Lane, who was looking at him in a speculative

fashion he didn't like at all. There was a question in the way his old friend's eyebrow and the corner of his mouth lifted in unison, but Irish ignored it.

"Let's get out of here," he said before Lane could make a comment about Mallory. "I'm not a fan of hanging around in funeral home parking lots."

Chapter Three

Based on a photo circulating, it seems the guest camping at the Suttons' house is a bona fide cowboy! Rumor has it he's an old friend of Lane Thompson's, so he'll probably be seen at Sutton's Place Brewery & Tavern. If you run into him at the taproom, make sure you say howdy and welcome him to town!

—*Stonefield Gazette* Facebook Page

"What were you thinking, letting him park that thing in our driveway?"

"Are you muttering about me under your breath, Mallory Sutton, or do you expect me to answer that?"

There had been little that annoyed her mother

more than the girls muttering things like that when they were growing up, but Mal was a grown woman and she'd mutter if she wanted to. "We don't know anything about him. We don't even know his actual *name*."

"He's a friend of Lane's," Ellen pointed out as she started pulling vegetables out of the fridge to make a salad. They closed the thrift shop early on Thursdays and Fridays so they could eat a very early dinner before opening the tavern, but whatever she'd been up to with Laura had put her mom a little behind schedule.

"He's a guy that Lane met a few times in a bar back when he was in college and has kept in touch with over the years. Lane doesn't know a lot about him, either."

"What's done is done. Unless he gives us good cause, I'm not asking him to move."

Was the power to raise the temperature a good twenty degrees just by looking at her good cause? "I know. I'm just grumbling."

"He sure is a handsome one." Her mother's tone had changed from sternly maternal to one of maternal matchmaking and Mal turned her back so she could roll her eyes.

She'd already gotten several text messages from Molly, who'd seen the picture of Mallory and Irish in the market and was annoyed she hadn't been at the funeral home to see him in person. Mallory wasn't mad about it, though. The last thing she needed was her best friend in the mix. Molly was a bright, upbeat ball of energy, but she didn't always have a great filter, especially when it came to Mallory's dating life.

"Please tell me you're going to have your way with that cowboy while he's in town," Evie said as she walked into the kitchen. Speaking of people with too much to say about her dating life, or lack thereof. "That is way too much man to let go to waste."

"Then maybe *you* should have your way with him."

"I can't. He's a friend of Lane's."

"Gwen is going to marry my ex-boyfriend," Mallory pointed out. "I thought we were past that fake rule at this point."

"You and Case dated when you were kids," Evie replied. "Lane is my ex-husband. It's a next-level rule. And Irish isn't really my type, but I bet he's yours. And he has a house on wheels out there. Knock on his door, scratch that itch and then do the shortest walk of shame ever."

"Evie!" Ellen tried to sound stern, but she didn't quite manage it because she was trying not to laugh.

"I don't need him to scratch any itch, thank you very much," Mallory said, even though it would only be fair, since he was the reason she *had* her current itch. "The boys will be home any minute. I'm going outside."

She didn't usually greet her sons in the driveway

after school, but her mother and younger sister were already on her last nerve and Irish hadn't even been there twenty-four hours. Keeping her own imagination in check was hard enough. She couldn't handle having theirs thrown in the mix, too.

While she waited for the boys to come up the sidewalk, she kept her back to the carriage house and camper, determined not to look for Irish. He was probably down in the brewing cellar with Lane anyway, she told herself—down the stairs separated from the taproom by a glass wall and a door Lane had coded with Evie's birthday, not realizing how much that would reveal about his feelings for his ex-wife when he forgot to change it before he had to share the code with them.

Luckily, she didn't have to wait long for the boys to turn the corner at the end of the street, and they waved when they saw her.

"Can we see inside the camper now?" Eli yelled as he ran up the driveway, dropping his backpack right in the middle of it.

"You said maybe later," Jack reminded her. His backpack joined his brother's, making a pile, and Mallory sighed. "It's later."

"I said *maybe later* because I wanted you to be quiet about it and go to school. But it's Mr. Irish's camper, which is like his home, and you can't just invite yourself in."

"It's just Irish," she heard that rich, low voice say

from behind her, and she took a second to let the wave of desire crash and recede before turning to face him.

"You won't even call my mother Ellen, so I think you get what I'm doing here," she pointed out.

"Mr. Irish," Eli said, much too loudly, "can we see your camper? I've never been in a camper before."

"Boys," Mallory snapped. "What did I just say about inviting yourself in?"

"It doesn't bother me," Irish said. "It's up to your mother, though."

Looking at the boys in front of her, silent but practically bouncing on their toes in excitement and looking at her with huge eyes, she sighed. "Are you sure you don't mind?"

"Not at all. But—" He looked at Jack and Eli, who stilled immediately. "First you have to pick up those backpacks and put them where they belong. When you're finished with anything else your mother tells you has to be done first, then I'll give you the grand tour."

When they picked up their backpacks and took off toward the house without so much as a grumble, Mallory rolled her eyes. "Well, aren't *you* the kid whisperer."

"It's only because they don't know me, and I have a deep voice. Give them a few days to figure out I'm not as scary as I look or sound, and they'll start ignoring me."

Somehow she didn't think so. There was authority in the way he spoke. He didn't raise his voice or sound aggressive at all, but there was an underlying matter-of-factness that didn't invite argument or negotiation—*this is what needs doing, so do it.*

They were back before Mallory standing in the driveway with Irish grew awkward and one of them had to come up with a reason to walk away.

"No homework?" Irish asked, looking skeptical.

"Nope," they said in unison.

"The elementary school teachers rarely give out weekend homework, so they're *probably* not fibbing," Mallory said, watching their faces for a guilty flush that didn't come.

"Let's go, then," he said, and they took off toward the camper as if seeing the inside of it was going to be the most exciting thing that had ever happened to them. At least they were easy to please, she thought as she followed along at a much slower pace.

The layout was simple enough. To the left of the door was the living space. A love seat across the back, under the window. The back wall, which bumped out, had dual recliners with cupholders and a small table with four chairs. There was a center island, which had the sink, as well as cabinets under the countertop, and the kitchen area was on the front wall. A TV set back over the gas fireplace was opposite the recliners.

She guessed his bedroom was to the right, divided

from the living space by two steps and a wall that had doors that looked like a closet or pantry. She didn't want to think about where he slept, so she focused on the living area.

She wasn't sure what she'd expected the camper to look like—maybe an adult version of the chaos Jack and Eli spread through the house if she didn't stay on them—but it wasn't this. The inside of the fifth-wheel was so clean, it would have looked as if he'd just picked it up from the dealer if not for slight signs of wear on the edges of the brown leather cushions and the beige carpet. Everything was put away and there wasn't even a dirty coffee mug in the sink.

"If we had a camper, it would look like a tornado went through it," she said, chuckling as she ran her hand over the spotless island counter.

"When you live in a bunkhouse, you don't really accumulate a lot of things because you don't have space for them. And if everybody doesn't pick up after themselves, there's trouble."

"Mom, look at this bed!" When she didn't answer right away because the thought of seeing where he slept had her looking anywhere but at Irish, Eli yelled again. "Mom! It's huge!"

Since there was no way out of seeing the huge bed that was going to add some detail to her wandering thoughts, Mallory went up the two steps leading to the master suite. The bathroom was first, but the door was closed and she didn't bother peeking in, even though she knew the boys probably had. Instead she stepped into the bedroom to find her sons sitting on the bed. She should probably tell them to get down, but the bed ate up most of the space and there wasn't a lot of room to navigate around it.

"It's not really huge," Irish said, and she was thankful he was behind her and couldn't see whatever her face did when that low voice spoke so close to her ear. He had to be close enough so, if she took a step back, she'd bump into him. "It's just a queen, and I'd prefer a king. I think it just looks big because it takes up all the space."

She nodded, not trusting herself to speak while processing the awareness that having Irish behind her and his bed in front of her might have made her do something reckless and ill-advised if her kids weren't in the room.

The bedroom was as neat as the rest of the camper, though there were a few personal effects on the nightstands. An alarm clock. A few books in a pile. She couldn't read the titles from where she stood, but they looked like historical fiction. On the other nightstand was a small laptop, plugged in to charge. The bed was made, of course. The comforter was a solid grayish-blue color and covered a mound that looked like two very hefty pillows.

When she caught herself wondering if those pillows smelled as good as the man who slept on them, Mallory knew it was time to leave. "Okay, boys. You saw the camper, but now we need to leave Mr. Irish in peace, and I have to get ready to open the tavern."

Their curiosity satisfied, they ran off toward the house, probably to tell their grandmother about the huge bed. Mallory climbed down the steps and moved out of Irish's way so he could close the door, intending to thank him for letting her sons invade his space, but he was looking at her intently. He wasn't quite frowning, but he definitely had something on his mind.

"Now that the boys are gone, I need to ask you a favor," he said, and she could hear the reluctance in his voice. "I know the whole *mister* thing is important to you, obviously. Yes, I have a hard time calling your mother by her first name. And I'll tolerate it if you insist, but I'm more comfortable with just plain Irish, even from the kids."

Questions swirled through her mind, but she could see an old hurt in his blue eyes, so she nodded and gave him a reassuring smile. "Of course. I'll let them know."

Just like that, the old pain was gone and he *almost* smiled. "Thank you. I guess I'll be hanging around the taproom later with Lane, so I'll see you, then."

"Great. See you later." She turned and hurried away before the heat climbing her neck could reach her cheeks and give away what she was thinking.

How she was going to get through a night of having him close enough to watch while she was supposed to be working was beyond her.

Irish was on his second beer of the night when Lane finally got a moment to pour himself a glass of water and lean against the bar to talk.

"This is quite a setup you've got." Irish wasn't easily impressed, but after getting a tour of Lane's brewing operation in the cellar and now seeing the tavern in action, he had to give credit where it was due.

"It wasn't easy." The look Lane gave him said that was an understatement. "But it was worth it. It breaks my heart a little every day that David didn't get to see it, but I think he'd be proud as hell."

"I'm sure he would be, and I hope *you* are, too."

"I am. Especially when I look around and see everybody relaxing with a beer, having a good time."

"Somebody should tell the people in this town that *howdy* isn't really a thing, though."

Lane laughed. "The *Gazette*'s Facebook Page gets a little out of hand now and then."

Irish held up the glass, which held an American wheat beer. "Not a very bold choice with this one."

"David wanted a brew for each of his daughters, and I brewed them from his notes. That one's Mallory's because it's light and can be paired with pretty much anything. As the middle child, she's always been the peacemaker and mediator of the family, so I guess it works."

Now Irish liked the beer even less. Of course it could be paired with anything. It was bland as hell. If a beer was going to be brewed in Mallory's honor, it should be rich and flavorful—full-bodied with depth and a spicy kick.

Lane went to the taps and then set two sample-sized glasses in front of him, pointing to each in turn. "Gwen's. And Evie's. You could stick around for a while, you know. I could use some help." Lane chuckled. "But I should tell you right up front that I can't pay you for your time. Not yet, anyway."

"Money's not really a concern," he said. Not only had he saved most of the wages he'd earned over his lifetime but his former boss had left him a nice nest egg in his will, which had only pissed off his useless son even more. The camper hadn't even put a dent in his bank account.

"It would be fun," Lane continued. "You've been talking about brewing for years. Stay here and actually do it for a while."

He shouldn't. He wanted to. Lane wasn't wrong about him having had the desire to brew beer for a long time. But if he stayed here longer than a few days, he was going to get himself in trouble with Mallory. The best kind of trouble, but trouble nonetheless. Plus, Mrs. Sutton didn't mind having a camper in her yard on a temporary basis, but he was sure she'd feel differently about him taking up residence there.

"I'll think about it," he said, not wanting to turn his friend down on the spot. It was better to let him feel like Irish had given it a lot of thought before hitting the road.

Somebody called Lane's name, so Irish was left to drink his beer and wait for a glimpse of Mallory. She was working in the kitchen and he wasn't sure if it was the norm for her or if she was hiding from him, but she'd barely come out of the small room off the bar.

He looked at the pale amber liquid in his glass, swirling it around a little. His first beer had been the house lager, of course, and it had been better than Irish had expected. Now he tasted the samples David Sutton had concocted for Mallory's sisters, who he'd met briefly tonight. There was no mistaking the three of them were sisters, with the eyes and the blond hair and just the general look of them, but neither of them were as pretty as Mallory.

Gwen, the oldest, was a writer who—according to Lane—had moved away to Vermont to write in peace, but when she'd come back to New Hampshire to help open the tavern, had fallen in love with Case Danforth. Her beer was an American imperial stout—strong and hearty, with a bit of a coffee taste to it. For Evie, the youngest, there was a pale ale that was bright and citrusy, almost bursting with flavor. It was a cheerful kind beer, perfect for fun things, like summer picnics.

He scowled at the bland wheat beer that was Mallory's and then drained the glass as she stepped out of the kitchen. She spoke to Lane, who was at the other end of the bar, for a few seconds and then headed for the door. But she glanced back at Irish before she opened it, and he wasn't sure if it was meant as an invitation or not, but he could use some air.

When he got outside, Mallory was standing by the corner of his camper, looking up at the sky. He noticed right away that she'd chosen a spot that wasn't visible from any of the tavern's windows, but he told himself that didn't necessarily mean anything.

She heard the door close and turned, her mouth curving into a smile when she saw him. "It's hot in that kitchen."

"Nice out here, though."

"I love spring. After a long, cold winter, it feels like a fresh start. We can be outside in the fresh air and everything will be blooming soon. I think spring is more my New Year than January 1."

The seasons had always mattered on the ranch, but it was about the work, not enjoying things. He liked that it wasn't that way for her. And he couldn't help wondering what it would be like to grow up as her sons were—free to run and enjoy things and play with the dog from across the street. By the time he was Jack's age, he was working his ass off, trying to save a farm that couldn't be saved beside a father who didn't deserve the help.

"What?" she asked, and he realized he'd been staring at her. He also realized he was close enough to touch her, and he didn't step back. But he wasn't very good at verbalizing what he was feeling, so he wasn't sure what to say, either.

Then she closed half the small amount of distance between them, and as she tilted her head to look up at him, he felt her fingers brush his. This was the moment to pull her into his arms—to kiss her until neither of them could remember their own names.

But he drew in a deep breath, trying to remember that no matter how badly he wanted to kiss her, it wasn't the right thing to do. "This is a bad idea. For you, I mean."

He lost the slight touch of her fingers as she stepped back until she bumped into the camper, confusion drawing her brows in. "Excuse me?"

"You don't want anything to do with a guy like me, Mallory." It hurt to say it out loud, even though it was the truth. "I'm not the settling-down kind. Hell, I live on wheels right now, and I'm a man with nothing to offer."

"Settling down? What are you talking about? Does a kiss mean something different in Montana, because that's all *I* was offering."

"I—"

"Wait. Because I have kids, you think I'm on some kind of a desperate quest to find myself another husband to be a father to them?"

Now that she was glaring at him with anger sparking in her dark eyes, he wasn't sure what to say. He'd only gotten involved with one single mother before, and it had become very clear very fast that a new husband and father for her children was exactly what she'd been looking for. And her kids had liked him, so unentangling himself had been messier than he ever wanted to go through again.

"Let me tell you something, cowboy," Mallory said, taking a step closer so she could jab a finger into his chest. Twice. "Wow. You really are all muscle."

He gave her a second to remember she was about to give him a dressing-down—verbally and not literally, unfortunately—but when she flattened her hand against his chest and her eyebrows arched, he knew it was up to him to get them back on track. "That's the something you wanted to tell me?"

"No." She looked up at him, but he was *very* aware she didn't remove her hand. "Being a single mother affects pretty much every aspect of my life, but it doesn't change the fact I'm a woman."

"There is *no* doubt about that."

"And just like a man who has children, a woman who has children can enjoy sex. She can have a one-night stand. A summer fling. A holiday hookup. Whatever she wants." She removed her hand from his chest so she could cross her arms. "And if that woman doesn't enjoy herself because she's thinking about all the stuff she has to do for her kids without help and the bills she has to pay on her own, then I guess maybe the man she's with just isn't good enough in bed to distract her."

She turned her back and had taken a few steps away from him before he was able to find his voice and call after her. "Is that a challenge?"

When she turned, her lips turned up in a regretful smile. "It's too bad you're leaving soon and I won't get a chance to know you better."

"Lane invited me to stick around for a while and help out," he said, enjoying the way her eyes widened and her cheeks flushed as his words sank in. "I think I'll do that."

Chapter Four

According to the public works department, a patch has been applied to the pothole on Fourth Street. The Stonefield police and fire departments would like it known, however, that while the pothole was admittedly a bad one, calling 911 to report it as a sinkhole was unnecessary.

—*Stonefield Gazette* Facebook Page

It wasn't even fully light yet when Mallory opened her eyes and stared at the ceiling with an unvoiced groan echoing around in her head.

Just shy of twenty-four hours ago, she'd found a cowboy out in her yard. And she was pretty sure that, last night, she'd challenged him to give her an orgasm. Never in her life had she been that forward, and she had no idea what had come over her. She couldn't even blame alcohol. There was just something about the man that had compelled her to let him know she was interested. Maybe it was the fact he was *supposed* to be leaving in a few days, which made him a safe bet for the fling she very much wanted to have with him.

Now, to top it all off, he was *not* leaving in a few days. No, Irish was going to stay and she was going to see him every single day for who knew how long, with that challenge hanging between them.

She pulled the blanket up over her head, letting a little of that inner groaning escape. Maybe when he'd said he was sticking around for a while, he meant an extra week. Possibly even two. It wasn't as though he could just stay indefinitely. Living in a camper in somebody's backyard wasn't a permanent thing.

A memory of her hand on his chest pushed its way to the forefront of her thoughts. Seeing his fully clothed body and watching him lift those heavy coolers onto his truck like they were nothing was one thing. But feeling that wall of muscle through the thin fabric of his shirt was another thing entirely.

Nope.

She was absolutely not going to hide in her bed and relive touching him. Though she might feel like a teenager with a crush at the moment, she actually wasn't and she needed to get up and get some stuff done. Preferably some physical labor that would expend enough energy over the day so she would go to sleep as soon her head hit the pillow tonight.

Throwing back the blanket, she forced herself into the shower, but as soon as the hot water started flowing over her body, she was imagining having Irish's naked body in there with her. Rather than beat her head against the tile, she deliberately started a mental to-do list that did *not* include doing anything with that particular man.

Clearly what she needed was a plan to keep herself busy. First, get the boys fed and across the street because Case had "hired" them to help him clean out his garage. His truck was always in the driveway, but now that Gwen had moved in, he wanted to clear out enough room so she could park her car inside. She had no doubt much of the stuff was going to end up at Sutton's Seconds and become *her* problem.

Then, since her mom was opening the thrift shop, Mallory would do some housework. Last summer, when they were all so focused on converting the carriage house into a taproom that the household stuff was suffering, her mom had actually hung a chore list in the kitchen, as though they were kids again. They'd complained about it, of course, but she had to admit it had worked.

She could check off a few things, and then head into town. Going to the store would get her through to early afternoon. Then she could be busy in the house or with the boys until she could hide herself away in the taproom kitchen. Hopefully it would be busy enough so there was good reason to stay in there and nobody would notice that she didn't come out and socialize with the customers.

Or with Irish.

But when a tiny sunshine-yellow convertible pulled into the driveway when she was halfway through vacuuming the throw rug in the living room, Mallory mentally scrapped the plan. Molly didn't always call or text before showing up—one of the perks of being her lifelong best friend and practically a daughter of the house—but she knew this wasn't a random visit. Molly wanted to meet Irish and there was no good reason why Mallory shouldn't be the one to introduce them.

The fact she was hiding from the man wasn't a good reason to offer. That would only lead to a lot of reasonable questions she didn't have reasonable answers to.

She'd managed to shove back her annoyance at having her Irish-avoidance plan foiled by the time Molly came through the front door, and even smiled. "Hey, Molly. I didn't know you were stopping by."

"I was in the neighborhood," Molly said, and they both laughed because pretty much anywhere in Stonefield was *in the neighborhood.* "I was going to come by the tavern last night and get a look at him, but my mom decided we needed to paint her office."

"Didn't you paint it last year?"

"Yes, we did. But Mom says the light gray it took her two months to pick out is boring and makes her sleepy."

Decorating and redecorating her office was something Amanda Cyrs put a lot of energy—and Molly's energy—into on a regular basis. Because it was the administrative office and clients never saw it, it was a space not bound by the classic elegance in the rest of the funeral parlor part of the house. "What color is it now?"

"Not light gray." Molly grinned and crossed her arms. "You tell me about your very attractive cowboy and I'll tell you what color we painted Mom's office last night."

"I don't understand why you want to meet him so badly," Mallory said, while simultaneously pulling out her phone and sending a text.

"Because you don't want me to, which means I *definitely* want to. You're practically vibrating with nervous energy right now, which is usual for me, but not for you. And I think all that nervous energy in you is because of him."

"You're ridiculous."

"No, what I am is the person who knows you the best—probably even better than your sisters—and this guy excites you, so I want to meet him."

Her phone buzzed in her hand, letting her know she'd gotten a response to her text. Grinning, she held up the photo Amanda had sent her. "This pale mint is beautiful, and perfect for your mom. And she loves it."

"You cheated." Molly took a step toward the door. "I guess I'll just pop over to the tavern and see if I can help at all."

"Molly. Don't you do it." Mallory gave her a stern-mom look that usually worked on her sons. Judging by the way Molly grinned and took another step, it wasn't as effective on best friends. "I mean it. You know they're probably locked in the cellar, anyway."

When the front door opened and Gwen walked in, Mallory sighed and looked up at the ceiling as if she could find some divine intervention there. Her older sister was carrying her massive tumbler with the Sutton's Place Brewery & Tavern decal on it and when she brought over coffee, it meant she was staying for a while.

"Hey, Molly," Gwen said. "I saw your car in the driveway, so I came over to say hi and see what everybody's up to."

"I'm trying to meet Mallory's cowboy."

"He's not *my* cowboy," Mallory said.

"What do you mean by *trying*?" Gwen asked, ignoring Mallory. "Isn't he here?"

"Mal has him locked in the cellar."

"I do not. I said he's probably in the brewing cellar with Lane and the door to the cellar happens to lock. You make it sound like I have him tied up in the basement." She could see by the look on their faces that both women were trying to come up with an inappropriate joke response, so she tried to change the subject. "Shouldn't you be writing, Gwen?"

"Probably." Her sister shrugged. "I'm in the percolating stage right now, and fresh air and walking around helps."

"Percolating? It's not coffee," she snapped.

Gwen took a sip of the coffee from her tumbler and then grinned. "It's my process and my process includes percolating. It's cute how you're trying to change the subject, though."

"Why would I care if Molly meets Irish? That doesn't even make sense."

"You tell us." Gwen gave her an expectant look, as if Mallory was actually going to respond to that—or even *could* respond to it.

"Fine." She may as well get it over with. "Let's go, then."

Irish was in deep now. Unable to resist the fire in Mallory's eyes when she'd tossed out what she probably *hadn't* meant as a challenge in bed, he'd committed to staying in Stonefield and he was too proud a man to take it back and drive away. That was one hundred percent what he *should* do.

But it wasn't necessarily what he *wanted* to do. If

he left now, he'd lose the chance to prove that, given the opportunity, he could make her forget everything. He really wanted to make Mallory forget everything except the feel of their bodies together.

"You look like you have something on your mind other than beer, my friend," Lane said, breaking into his thoughts. He'd never been more thankful that he wasn't an expressive person by nature, so he probably didn't look *too* guilty about the direction his thoughts had been going.

"That happens occasionally." Though it was a little odd to be thinking about something other than beer when they were in the process of sampling a batch.

"The only thing better than thinking about beer is thinking about a woman," Lane said, and Irish could tell by his tone that he was fishing.

It wasn't in Irish's nature to sit around talking about feelings with other guys, but he considered Lane a friend. And Lane considered Mallory to be like family. If Lane didn't like the idea of his former sister-in-law hooking up with a guy like Irish, things could get really messy and he didn't want that.

"Where is those kids' dad?" he finally asked, figuring it was kind of an admission of his interest in Mallory without coming out and saying it. He was also curious what the chances were a jealous ex would take exception to Irish's presence. Not that he was worried, but it didn't hurt to know in advance. "Why isn't he around?"

"Mallory and Jeff have been divorced for a long time."

"I get that, but did the guy just take off after the divorce? It's the weekend, so I figured there'd be a visit with the dad, but nobody's mentioned it."

"He's out of the picture." There was a lot more to the story, but judging by the way Lane's expression closed off, he wasn't going to get it from him. Not that it mattered.

Irish had no use for a man who walked away from his children. That was enough for him to write a person off, no questions asked. But he also wondered what kind of guy would be lucky enough to have Mallory and then walk away from her.

The worst kind of fool—that was who.

As much as he'd like to know the full story, he respected Lane for not spilling everything he knew about Mallory's marriage. And he probably knew *everything*, since he'd not only been married to Evie, but had been good friends with David Sutton. It wasn't easy to find people you could trust to know when to gossip and when not to, and he liked knowing his friend was on the right side of that fence.

Lane's phone dinged—but a doorbell sound rather than the more common chime—and he muttered under his breath as he fished it out of his pocket.

"That sound means one or more of the Sutton women want to bug me about something."

Irish had one of those rugged flip phones because it fit in his pocket and stood up to the abuse it took, but it made texting a pain in the ass. He'd never cared, since he rarely used it, but as he watched Lane reading his screen, he thought it might be kind of nice to have one of the Sutton women in particular bugging him about things.

"You're being summoned," Lane told him, grinning as he slid the phone back into his pocket.

"Me? What do they want me for?"

"Molly wants to meet you."

"Mallory's friend, with the funeral home?" That was interesting. What had Mallory said about him that had brought her best friend over to meet him?

"You'll like Molly. Everybody does. And they're in the taproom now, so good luck."

"I could just hide down here. You could say you don't know where I am."

Lane chuckled. "They know you're here because your truck is hard to miss in the driveway and where else would you be? And they know the pass code to the door, so you wouldn't get much of a reprieve anyway."

"Come up with me. At least I won't be outnumbered."

This time Lane laughed out loud at him. "Not a chance. I'm working."

"You're drinking beer."

"No, my friend. I'm testing samples and taking notes. That makes it very important work that I can't possibly take a break from right now."

Rather than admit the idea of going upstairs so Mallory could introduce him to her best friend had his stomach tied up in knots, Irish snorted and headed for the stairs.

Because the wall separating the staircase from the taproom was glass, he could see them once he cleared two-thirds of the steps. They had their backs to him, so he had a moment to watch them before the opening door would get their attention. Unlike Mallory and Gwen—who was also with them—Molly had long dark hair, pulled back into a sleek ponytail. She was a little taller and slimmer than the two sisters, too.

Just as he reached to open the door, Mallory turned slightly and looked over her shoulder, as if she could sense him watching her. Their gazes locked and he was overwhelmed again by the feeling that there was something between them—something that didn't make sense and that he couldn't explain, but that went well beyond just thinking the other was attractive.

Then the other women turned and he had no choice but to step out from behind the glass—taking off his hat as he did—and try not to feel too awkward as Mallory introduced him to her best friend.

"Well," Molly said, and after she gave him a thorough looking-over, she grinned. "Howdy, cowboy."

"Nice to meet you, ma'am," he said, ignoring the entire howdy thing.

"Ma'am?" Molly laughed and gave Mallory a questioning look.

She shrugged. "It's a thing he does."

"He looks very stern," Molly said in a stage whisper.

"Also a thing he does," Gwen said, earning her a look from Mallory.

No, this wasn't awkward at all, Irish thought. Since the introductions were over, he settled his hat back on his head and tried to think of something to say to the three women who were looking at him as if waiting for him to talk.

"I should get back down there," he said, since he couldn't think of anything else. "I'm helping Lane out with…testing."

"In other words, we interrupted them drinking beer," Gwen said, clearly amused.

"It's part of the process," Mallory replied, and he liked that she came to his defense so quickly. "We'll let you get back to it."

He tipped his hat in farewell, which got a dreamy sigh from Molly, and started to turn back to the glass door. Regretting not having kept his foot in it to keep it from latching to hasten his escape, he was about to punch in the code when Mallory spoke.

"Oh, Irish?" He turned back to face her, thankful the other two women were halfway to the front door. “We eat an early dinner on the days the tavern’s open. My mom will probably expect you to be there.”

He shook his head. She smiled and nodded. He sighed.

“I’ll let you know what time,” she said, and then he once again got the pleasure of watching her walk away.

Chapter Five

If you stop by Sutton's Place Brewery & Tavern or Sutton's Seconds this Sunday and see Ellen Sutton, don't forget to wish her a happy birthday! Because she runs two businesses now, she'll be celebrating with her family on Monday, when they're both closed, and we know she's thrilled that all three of her daughters are here in Stonefield this year!

—*Stonefield Gazette* Facebook Page

Mallory wasn't sure what had possessed her to invite Irish to eat dinner with them. And she was using the term *invite* loosely. She'd more or less told him he had no choice, and now she was the one suffering because her mother had sat their guest next to Mallory and he was a big man who took up a lot of space.

There was a lot of brushing of body parts going on, and she was afraid she was going to just burst into flames right there at the kitchen table.

Him joining them for dinner was meant to be payback for not leaving the way he was supposed to. If she'd known Lane had asked him to stay in Stonefield for a while, she never would have said all that about a man needing to be good enough in bed to make her forget everything going on in her hectic life.

"Mal, are you okay?" her mom asked, and Mallory wished she could just sort of melt off her chair and into a puddle under the table like a cartoon character. "You look flushed, honey."

"I'm fine," she said, but then the length of Irish's calf pressed against hers and she had no doubt it was deliberate.

Ellen frowned. "You made it through the whole winter without getting sick. I hope you're not coming down with something now."

The only thing Mallory was coming down with was a serious case of liking pretty much any part of Irish's body touching any part of *her* body, but she certainly wasn't going to confess that at the family dinner table.

"You can't be sick tonight," Evie said. "I have

to help Gwen, so you need to help Lane handle the taproom."

"You can't help Gwen another time?"

"Nope. Her publicist talked her into doing a Facebook Live thing to keep up interest in her books and you know how Gwen is with social media. I need to be there for tech support and also to make sure she doesn't miss any questions or anything."

Mallory sighed. "There are three nights a week when the tavern's closed, but whatever. I'm sure I can handle the kitchen and the dishes *and* play bartender on a Saturday night."

"I can help," Ellen said. "Case would probably be willing to keep an eye on the boys, since Gwen will be busy."

"I can handle the bar with Lane," Irish said quietly, and Mallory could practically feel the tension in him ratchet up as they all turned to look at him.

She probably shouldn't have been surprised by the offer. He struck her as the kind of guy who believed if there was a job to be done, you just did it. And he wasn't going to let her mother do a job he could do instead. But being a bartender, especially in a local-heavy taproom like theirs, was a very social job and that seemed to be something he struggled with.

"Or I can do dishes," he continued. "Whatever needs doing."

He absolutely couldn't help in the kitchen. It was a small space and there was no way Mallory's nerves could handle bumping into him and brushing against him all night. It was hard to picture the strong, stern cowboy behind the bar, but it wasn't hard at all to imagine what that kind of physical proximity would feel like, and that *was* a problem.

"You don't have to do that," Ellen said. "You're a guest."

"I appreciate that, ma'am, but I prefer to earn my keep."

Even though he said it quietly and with respect, he had a way of making the words that came out of his mouth sound like a done deal, so Mallory wasn't surprised when her mother smiled and nodded.

"I think our customers would love seeing you behind the bar tonight."

A few hours later, Mallory had to admit her mother had been right. The Sutton's Place regulars loved Irish. They all greeted him with a "howdy," which she had to admit he accepted with a lot more patience than she would have. And she never would have guessed the residents of Stonefield would have so many questions about ranch life, but they kept up a steady stream of them. Mostly they wanted to know if a detail they'd seen in this show or that movie was authentic, and he didn't seem to mind weighing in.

"The guy's a natural," Lane said during one of his frequent visits to the kitchen with yet more dirty glasses. "I've had to empty the tip jar twice already because they're filling it that fast."

"He's like a new toy they can't get enough of. But eventually they'll get used to him and he'll be just another toy in the toy box."

"If they're going to keep tipping like this, I hope he doesn't end up at the bottom of the toy box anytime soon."

She laughed and held out a plate of pretzel bites with beer cheese to take out to a customer. Those were even more popular than the nachos, and she made a note on the clipboard hanging on the wall to double their next order.

"Why don't you take those out and I'll take a turn in the kitchen," Lane said. "You've been in here all night. Go move around, talk to some people."

She was about to shake her head and tell him she was absolutely fine where she was, but the others taking turns in the kitchen now and then so she could have a turn at the fun jobs was how they did things. And she was reluctant to admit that she didn't want to leave the kitchen because she was hiding from Irish.

"Thanks," she said, setting the pretzel bites down so she could take off the big apron she wore to protect her clothes. Then she picked up the plate and, after taking a deep breath, stepped out of the kitchen.

She almost walked right into Irish. She hadn't realized he was at this end of the bar, and thinking about the conversation she'd just had with Lane made her wince. Hopefully he hadn't heard her talking about him as if he was just a new toy everybody would grow tired of. It had been a poor analogy for describing how their customers felt about having a real cowboy behind the bar.

But when he turned to face her, Mallory didn't read anything in his expression but pleasure at seeing her.

"They let you out," he said in that low voice that never failed to make her shiver.

"It's nice to get out of the kitchen for a few minutes here and there." She would have been content to stand there and drown in the intensity of his eyes for the rest of the night, but she was still holding the pretzel bites. "I need to deliver these, but I'll be back."

"I'll be here."

Yes he would, she thought as she made her way through the tables to deliver the pretzel bites to the far corner. After dropping them off, she greeted a few people as she made her way to the popcorn machine and started a fresh batch. They went through a lot of popcorn, but Case had been right to urge them to look into buying a used machine. People who ate a lot of popcorn got very thirsty and bought more beer.

It didn't take her very long, and then she was back behind the bar, where Irish was punching holes in the authenticity of one of a customer's favorite Western movies.

"So you don't sing the cows lullabies every night

so they'll go to sleep?" Ricky asked, sounding genuinely disappointed.

"I guess if you're driving cattle and bed them down for the night, singing can help keep them calm and maybe mask some small noises that might spook them into a stampede," Irish said, and Mallory wondered if that was the truth or if Irish just felt bad about bursting Ricky's bubble. "But on the ranch, we don't go out every night and sing them lullabies."

"Oh."

"I've been told that singing in the barn makes dairy cows give more milk, though." Irish tipped his head slightly, which she'd figured out was his version of shrugging his shoulders. "I guess singing to cows is a good thing."

Visibly cheered, Ricky pushed his empty glass toward Irish. "I'll have one more."

While Irish took care of his customer, Mallory cashed out a couple who were ready to leave. After clearing their glasses and wiping down the bar where they'd been sitting, there was nothing left to do. The other customers were all content and chatting with each other and, short of going back into the kitchen, she was out of busywork to distract her.

With nothing else to occupy her hands, she fiddled with the glasses that lined shelves along the wall. One of Evie's ideas was to etch the names of regulars into their very own Sutton's Place glass, under the logo, to increase their sense of belonging.

It had been a great idea—the customers loved it—but sometimes their alphabetical order got messed up and if the glasses were shelved in a hurry with the logo and name not facing front, it could take time to find the right one.

Then Irish stepped up next to her and the calming effect of switching two misplaced glasses was immediately displaced by her desire to lean into the way his closeness overwhelmed her senses.

"I can't figure you out," he said in a voice so quiet, she could barely hear him. There was no chance anybody else would.

"What do you mean?"

"You know what I mean."

Even though his voice was still low, those five words had a husky quality that left no doubt what he was talking about. And it made sense that he wouldn't be able to figure her out, since she'd done nothing but send some very mixed signals since he arrived. Not only was that not fair to him, but it made everything awkward.

"I thought you were only here for a few days," she admitted in a whisper. "It's a lot more complicated now."

"If me being here is a problem for you in any way, or makes you uncomfortable, I can move on. I saw Lane's setup, which is why I stopped by, and there's still an ocean for me to see."

"No." The word was out of her mouth before she

could even process whether Irish moving on would be a good idea. And even though she knew that response had come from a body part other than her head, she couldn't bring herself to take it back. "I don't want you to leave. I just need to...cool things off, I guess."

"Okay." He reached out to turn one of the glasses so the name could be read. "If you change your mind—about me leaving *or* cooling things off—just let me know."

She nodded, not trusting herself to speak when his deliciously bare, muscular forearm was in her line of sight. Most of his shirts had long sleeves, but tonight he'd borrowed one of the blue Sutton's Place T-shirts they'd had made from Lane. The way it hugged his chest and back was bad enough, but those forearms on display were killing her. How was she supposed to cool off when everything about him tempted her?

"Hey, Irish," Ricky called. "When you castrate the cows, do you really eat their testicles?"

Mallory was close enough to hear the curse word Irish muttered under his breath, and she had to cover her amusement with a cough. The question was a decent substitute for a cold shower, though she knew the effect would be temporary.

Ricky pulling Irish's attention away from her gave Mallory the perfect opportunity to slip back into the kitchen, and she took it. While it was nice to be behind the bar once in a while, the only way she was going to keep things cool between her and Irish was distance.

As much distance as she could manage from a man living in her backyard.

Irish wasn't accustomed to feeling out of his element. He was comfortable in his own skin, always knew what he was supposed to be doing and didn't really care what anybody else was up to. He kept his mind on his work and, for most of his life, his work had filled all of his time.

He'd intended to stop in New Hampshire for a couple of days and check out Lane's brewing operation. He hadn't seen the guy in a long time, but they'd kept in touch and he was curious to see what all the talk over the years had come to. Then he was going to continue east until he hit the ocean and, once he'd seen that for the first time, head back west to...somewhere. He'd even thought about checking out some ranches in Texas because that was the work he knew, but at least it was a hell of a lot warmer in the winter. He had figured he'd come up with a destination after he'd pointed his truck west.

Instead, he was in the middle of Mrs. Sutton's birthday barbecue, surrounded by a family that didn't seem to care they'd only known him for a few days. They were determined to make him feel at home, surrounded by Suttons.

The exception was Case Danforth. Case was nice

enough, but he wasn't quite as openly welcoming as the rest of them were. He obviously had some reservations about a guy Lane had met years ago showing up out of the blue and setting up camp in the Suttons' backyard.

Irish liked that about him.

He also liked Case's dog, Boomer, who was a German-shepherd-and-black-Lab mix. Irish was a dog lover, and he was pretty sure Boomer taking to him quickly was a point in his favor as far as Case was concerned.

But Irish knew that point could be canceled out in a hurry if Case caught on to the fact he was having some *very* impure thoughts about the man's future sister-in-law, so he was using every bit of his considerable willpower to keep his eyes off of Mallory.

It wasn't easy. Mallory was constantly on the move and his gaze just naturally seemed to find her. And he could look away, but then her voice or her laugh would draw his attention again. She wanted to cool things down between them and he didn't think that was possible, but he would do his part. If and when she got tired of fighting the chemistry pulling at them, she'd let him know. It would be her move.

What he needed to do was put the words he'd overheard her saying to Lane—*just another toy in the toy box*—on a constant loop in his head so he wouldn't forget that, while he might be a fun new toy to play with, eventually he'd get kicked under the bed.

In an effort to distract himself, Irish went to the gazebo to get a second helping of pasta salad. Mrs. Sutton had told him that before she and her husband had bought the property, it had been an upscale inn, which probably helped explain why the carriage house they'd converted into the brewery and taproom was so large.

And there was also a massive gazebo in the backyard, overlooking the river. Mrs. Sutton had said the previous owners hosted weddings and other special occasions in it, but her husband had put a long picnic table in it. Irish liked the space and the shade, and he really liked the pasta salad.

He only had a few moments alone, though, before Case joined him in the gazebo with Boomer at his heels.

"Laura makes a mean pasta salad," Case said after a glance at Irish's plate. Then he took the lid off the bowl—which was one of four different dishes that were sitting in a long pan of ice—and dumped a big spoonful on a fresh plate.

"It's good stuff," Irish agreed. He looked out at the people milling around the yard, playing a game they called cornhole or sitting in groups chatting until he found the woman he'd been introduced to earlier as Laura Thompson. She was Lane's mother and Case's aunt, and she handled the office work for their tree service, as she'd done for her husband and brother-in-law. She was also one of Mrs. Sutton's best friends.

There had been a lot of new faces over the past few days, but Laura's pasta salad would definitely ensure her name stuck in his head.

"Lane tells me you'll be sticking around for a while," Case said, his tone casual.

"Yup." He would have left it at that because he usually didn't feel a need to explain himself to anybody, but he knew the guy was just looking out for a house full of women he cared about a lot. "I don't really have anywhere I need to be and Lane and I have talked about brewing beer for a lot of years, so I'll hang out with him for a little while before I move on."

"I'm glad you were able to get out here. Lane's mentioned you over the years, so I know it means a lot to him that you came to see what he's done."

"He told me you did a lot of work on the taproom. It's a great space."

Case nodded. "Thanks. We all worked our asses off after David passed away, but it was worth it. And we had to hire a couple more guys for the tree service and they're good workers, but it's nice to have some of Lane's focus back on that business."

Irish nodded, because he wasn't sure what else to say to the man, and he shoved a forkful of pasta salad into his mouth to give him an excuse to remain silent.

"Anyway, I'm going to see if there are any burgers left," Case said. "If you need anything, just give a shout. Literally, even, since I live right across the street. And hell, Boomer loves to get on the couch and watch for the boys, so you could just whistle."

Case injected a lot of humor into the words while scratching behind his dog's ear, but Irish heard the subtle warning. The women weren't really alone. Case was watching him. And so was Boomer.

An hour later, Irish got sucked into playing a game of cornhole with Jack. It involved tossing a bean bag sack at a board with a hole in it, and trying to land the sack in the hole. It was like horseshoes, so he got the hang of it quickly, especially with Eli coaching him as though he was training Irish for the cornhole Olympics.

"Just so you know," Mrs. Sutton said as she walked past with a pitcher of lemonade, "they never stop. Feel free to quit on them anytime."

"Yes, ma'am," he said, thinking a glass of lemonade would be perfect right about then, but she'd taken the pitcher to where a bunch of them were sitting around in camp chairs, chatting.

He wasn't much for sitting around. Or chatting.

But a few minutes later, he surrendered to his thirst and bowed out of the game. He thought maybe he could sneak up to the small table near Mrs. Sutton's chair, take one of the plastic cups from the small stack and make his escape with lemonade without interrupting the conversation, but no such luck.

"Irish," she said, clearly pleased that he'd joined them. "Have a seat and visit with us for a while."

Of course the only empty chair was between Mallory and Gwen. Evie had been sitting in it earlier, but he didn't see her now. "Yes, ma'am."

He sat and then took a long drink of the sweet lemonade because not only was he thirsty, but sitting so close to Mallory with an audience that included her mother made his mouth go dry.

"So Irish, you and Lane met at a bar in Montana?" Ellen asked, and he knew she was just trying to draw him into conversation since she already knew they had.

"Yes, ma'am."

She watched him for a few seconds and then her eyes crinkled as her smile widened. "Let me rephrase that into something that's not a yes-or-no question. Tell me the story of how you and Lane met."

"Yes, ma'am. It's quite a story." He paused a moment for effect. "We met at a bar in Montana."

He was grateful she laughed—that she'd caught that he was trying to be funny—and he liked all the laughter around them. Mallory's, especially. All four of the Sutton women had great laughs, and it was clear to him they laughed a lot, but he was definitely particular to the middle sister's.

Once the laughter faded, he finished the story. "I'd been to the city for some reason—a cattle auction, maybe—and stopped at a bar I knew on the way home. There was a kid with a college sweatshirt and a really funny accent sitting at the bar, and I saw him holding up his glass to really look at one of the local brews. He asked the bartender a few questions and then I asked one and then we got to talking about brewing."

"Lane has an accent?" Gwen asked, and the women laughed again.

He wished he was sitting across from Mallory rather than next to her. Not only because his body was so hyperaware of the proximity of *her* body, which made it hard to concentrate, but because he couldn't see her face. He liked watching her laugh, and he couldn't really do that from the seat next to hers.

Belatedly, he realized it might not have been a great idea to sit with a group of women, even for the lemonade. The boys were still playing cornhole, and Lane and Case were looking at one of the trees lining the back of the yard. Lane was pointing at one of the larger limbs, so he assumed they were talking about needing to do some cutting. And he was alone, surrounded by women who might not be shy about asking him questions that were harder to answer than how he'd met Lane.

He wasn't used to talking about himself. Not that he had any deep, dark secrets. He simply hadn't had the kind of life that was worth talking about, unless you wanted to know about running a ranch. And sure, he'd seen his share of hilarious mishaps over the years, but they were bunkhouse stories and not really for this audience.

Luckily, Laura mentioned an item in the thrift shop she had her eye on, which turned the conversation in that direction. Irish listened, not wanting to appear rude by getting up and walking away while they were talking, but he wasn't totally comfortable.

It was strange that the Sutton family and their friends could make him feel so at home, while also making him feel as though he'd never belonged anywhere less than he did here.

Chapter Six

The public works department has replaced the High Street sign yet again. (We've lost count of how many times it has been stolen.) Thanks to the unexpected skill some Stonefield residents have shown in concocting disguises, the cameras put in place haven't been effective, and the prospect of changing the street's name will be discussed at the next selectmen's meeting.

—*Stonefield Gazette* Facebook Page

"What's going on out there?"

Mallory startled so hard, she dropped the knife she'd been using to cut up lemons. Luckily, she'd been staring out the window instead of actually slicing, or she might have cut herself. She'd been so lost in watching Irish lift heavy rocks she hadn't heard her mother come into the kitchen. "Nothing."

"You were on your tiptoes trying to see *something.*"

She'd had to stand on her toes in order to see the corner of the yard Irish was in, but she wasn't going to admit that. Thankfully, she wasn't sure her mother was tall enough to get the same view, and Irish was finishing up. She wouldn't have to explain that she'd been tormenting herself by watching the walking temptation she was denying herself.

It had been a week since she told Irish she needed for things to cool off between them. She had regrets.

"I was just looking to see how the rock wall was coming along," Mallory confessed, since she had to say something believable, and there was a chance her mom knew Irish had been out there. She chose not to confess that her interest in the rock wall was mostly due to the man building it.

"It looks good, and hopefully it'll serve its purpose. I'm glad it will be done before things start greening up."

Its purpose being to protect the garden bed it was bordering. They all tended to cut across the end of the bed while walking through the yard and the boys seemed oblivious to it when riding their bikes, so the edges between lawn and garden bed had grown ragged.

Mallory chuckled. "Those are some big rocks. I think in garden versus bikes, the flowers will be winning this summer."

"It's so sweet of Irish to help us out with the rocks. I keep telling him he's our guest, but he keeps telling me he doesn't mind and that he prefers to earn his keep."

"I think he comes from a life where you get room and board along with your wages in exchange for hard work. I don't think he knows how to sit and do nothing."

"It's pretty warm for April," her mother said. "You should take him some lemonade."

"I think he's done," Mallory replied, and when she saw the little smile on her mother's face, she realized she'd just confessed she'd been watching him work. "I saw him loading more rocks into the wheelbarrow."

Because they hadn't known how long it would take them to build the stone wall around the garden bed, they'd had the load of wall-worthy rocks dumped in a corner of the driveway to keep them out of the way. It hadn't taken them but a few trips to realize they should have just gone with a little border fence. But it was important to her mom that it match the stone walls bordering the rest of the property, so they placed a few rocks whenever they had the time and ambition.

Irish had already done more in a few hours than they'd done since the delivery in early March, so a glass of lemonade was definitely in order. She just didn't want to be the one to bring it to him.

"I'm cutting up lemons for a new batch," Mallory said, concentrating on giving away nothing with her tone or expression. "But you could bring him a glass."

"I'll finish that," her mother said, picking up the knife before Mallory could object. "It's a beautiful day. Go get some fresh air and then you can help me remake my bed."

They usually did the larger household chores and the grocery shopping on Mondays, when the thrift shop was closed and the boys were in school. Cutting up lemons certainly hadn't been on the list, but it had been something she could do in front of the kitchen window.

"You gave him a whole gallon of lemonade to keep in his camper," Mallory reminded her, looking for any reason to get out of going outside that didn't involve confessing why she didn't want to. "If he's thirsty, he'll get some."

"Irish is saving us from doing a lot of hard physical labor, Mallory. Take the man a glass of lemonade."

That wasn't intended as a suggestion, so Mallory washed her hands and poured a tall glass of lemonade. Stripping beds and scrubbing bathrooms had her hair coming out of its messy bun and throwing a zip-up hoodie on didn't dress up the fact she was wearing an old T-shirt over yoga pants. It was funny how she hadn't cared at all when she was on her way to the market, but now it was only her mother's presence that kept her from detouring to her bedroom to clean up a bit before going outside.

She was halfway across the yard when Irish set the wheelbarrow handles down and then took off his hat to run his hand through his hair. Then he lifted the hem of his T-shirt, gathering it in both hands, and hauled it up to wipe the sweat from his face with the fabric.

Mallory's mouth went dry as the rising T-shirt revealed the tight, hard ripples of his stomach. Irish was a big man, but he certainly wasn't soft. She'd stopped walking and she knew she should start moving again because it would be embarrassing if he turned and caught her standing there, staring at his abs.

It was hard to look away, though. And she knew she was going to spend a lot of time in the near future imagining what those rippled muscles would feel like under her hands. As he dropped the shirt, she managed to force her gaze back above his neck and made her feet move, but it wasn't easy.

She almost tripped over the grass when he noticed her approaching and heat flared in his eyes. The way he kept looking at her—as if he was imagining her as naked as she liked to imagine him—didn't help her at all when it came to her determination to cool things off.

"I brought you some lemonade," she said, holding the glass out to him.

"I'm glad that's for me. I was afraid you were going to stand in front of me and drink it."

Even though his expression gave away nothing, she'd come to recognize the teasing tone of his voice and the way his eyes squinted slightly, as though he was smiling without his mouth moving. She would have laughed, but his fingers brushed hers as he took the glass from her, and how ridiculous was she that just that little bit of contact was enough to rob of her of all coherent thought?

He drained half the glass while she looked everywhere but at the way his throat worked while he swallowed. After giving a contended sigh, he focused those blue eyes that haunted her dreams back on her.

"Thank you. I needed that."

"It's not usually this hot in April. And we really appreciate you doing this. You're going a lot faster than we would have."

He tilted his head slightly to show it wasn't a big deal to him. "Did you know there are some boxes on the bar in there?"

She nodded. "It's stuff from the thrift shop. Sometimes we get things that will get a higher price online than selling them locally, but I have to photograph the stuff and write descriptions and all that. I like to take the pictures in the taproom because the bar surface is actually nicer than our table in the house, plus I can get peace and quiet if I wait until after dinner so my mom can be with the boys in the house. I'll probably do those tonight."

"When do you get time for yourself?"

The mirthless laugh escaped her lips before she could stop it. She didn't like to complain, mostly because it wouldn't do any good, but also because wallowing in self-pity wouldn't get anything done. "I'm raising two very active little boys and I'm running two businesses with my mother—one of which is a bar that's open until almost my bedtime. Monday is our *free* day, which means it's packed with errands and chores. I get time for myself when I'm sleeping."

"But you don't really get to enjoy it because you're asleep."

That comment wasn't entirely accurate because she'd had some pretty steamy dreams lately, and she'd enjoyed them immensely. "I don't get a lot of time to myself, no. But I'm not going to complain because I get to raise my sons in the beautiful home I grew up in, surrounded by an amazing support system, especially with Evie and Gwen around now. And I appreciate the flexibility working with my mom gives me because one of us can always be around for the boys. I don't get a lot of time to myself, but my life could be a *lot* harder."

He nodded. "That's a good way to look at things."

It was, though lately she'd found herself wishing for just a *little* more time to herself. An hour would do it—an hour alone with Irish, without worrying about her family or how they might take it. No matchmaking, no taking into consideration whether or not her sons were getting too attached to him. Just the two of them for a single hour.

After finishing off the lemonade, he handed the empty glass back to her. "I appreciate it."

"No problem. Just shout if you want more. Or come in and help yourself." She was out of reasons to stand there with him, so she smiled. "I'll let you get back to work, I guess."

"I'll see you later," he said in that way that always sounded like a promise.

She'd never been more self-conscious about how her butt looked in the yoga pants she was wearing than when she made her way back to the house because she was fairly certain he was watching her walk away. Or at least she hoped so.

It wasn't hard for Irish to come up with a reason to be in the brewing cellar after supper. There had been a big grain delivery, and even with Case's help, it had taken him and Lane quite a while to get it all put away properly in the storage room. The hard part was coming up with a reason for him to stay once Lane was ready to go home for the night.

If he knew Mallory, she'd wait until they were done so she didn't get in the way or make them feel as if they should stay and help her. He *wanted* to stay, but he didn't want Lane around while he helped her. He wanted to be alone with her while not standing in the damn yard.

He resorted to "forgetting" his cell phone.

He wasn't proud of it, but if it got him a few minutes alone with Mallory, it was worth it. After taking it out of his pocket with the excuse of checking the time, he held it in his hands for a few minutes before setting it down on the edge of the oversize sink. He washed his hands and then just walked away, leaving the phone there.

Once Lane was finished for the night, they walked out together and Irish talked to him briefly through Lane's open truck window. Then, just as Lane was about to pull away, Irish patted his pocket.

"Damn. Left my cell phone down there."

As planned, a tired working man in motion toward his home and bed wanted to stay in motion. "You know the code. I'll see you tomorrow."

He didn't have long to wait before he heard a thump on the floor over his head and knew his plan had been a success. Well, the first half of it, anyway. Now it was time to see how the second half would play out.

Making sure his footsteps were heavy on the wooden stairs so he wouldn't scare Mallory, he left the cellar with his cell phone in hand. She was alone, not a mother or sister in sight, and he breathed a sigh of relief.

"I left my phone downstairs," he said once he'd closed the glass door behind him, holding it up so she could see the evidence.

"I haven't seen you use it a single time since you've been here, so I'm surprised you missed it." She pulled open the flaps of the first box sitting on the bar and sighed.

"Doing this all by yourself?"

"I don't mind. Mom's with the boys and Evie decided we should have a ladies' night to kick off school vacation week, so she's creating some social media graphics."

"You'd probably sell more beer if you have a ladies' night at the end of vacation week, to celebrate surviving it."

She laughed, and he soaked in the sound. He missed the sound of her voice—especially her laughter—every hour he wasn't with her. "The diner's been doing free desserts for parents at the end of vacation week for years. We didn't want to step on that."

"Let me help you with this," he said, gesturing at the box.

"You spent most of the day working on our stone wall and then the rest of it helping Lane and Case with the delivery. I think we've gotten more than our fair share of free labor out of you today."

"I wouldn't call it free labor, exactly. Your mother won't accept any rent for my camper being parked here and she keeps feeding me, so—"

"Yes, I know. You prefer to earn your keep."

"You say that like it's a bad thing."

"No." She sighed and pulled an item wrapped in tissue paper out of the box. "Of course it's not a bad thing. I just hope you know we're getting the better end of the bargain."

"Moving some rocks around in exchange for getting to see you every day is a pretty good deal in my book."

She looked at him, the impact of her pretty blue eyes stealing his breath. He could drown in them, except he got distracted by the pink flush that climbed her neck and warmed her cheeks. Her lips parted slightly, and her breaths were shorter and faster than usual.

Irish wanted to kiss her more than he'd ever wanted to do anything else in his life. "If you were serious about wanting to cool things off between us, you really need to stop looking at me like that."

She blinked. "I was serious."

He knew that. But he also knew that what she thought she should do and what she wanted to do were two very different things.

"I'm not going to be able to resist you much longer, though," she added, and her words lit a fuse within him. If he didn't get to kiss her soon, he might actually explode.

He cleared his throat. "Do you want me to pretend to look disappointed?"

She laughed and pushed playfully at his shoulder. "How would I even tell? Would your expression actually change?"

"Of course it would. When I'm disappointed my eyebrows and mustache drop a fraction of an inch or so."

"Ah, that's what that expression is. I guess that means you were disappointed in the New England boiled dinner we had for supper last night."

"It has no flavor. I've never eaten a food that actually tastes like nothing before." Too late, he realized he could have expressed that sentiment with a little more tact. He didn't eat every meal with the Sutton family, despite Mrs. Sutton's urging to do just that, but he'd let slip he'd never had a New England boiled dinner and she'd been insistent. He should have tried harder to get out of it.

Fortunately, Mallory looked more amused than offended. "It's definitely a meal that requires a lot of butter and pepper."

He thought it would take a lot more than butter and pepper to give that meal a flavor, but he didn't want to talk about ham and cabbage anymore. He wanted to go back to the *I'm not going to be able to resist you much longer* thread and tug on that a bit more.

Moving slightly behind and closer to her, so his shoulder was behind hers, he leaned in. "Why are you trying so hard to resist me if you think it's a lost cause?"

She shivered when his breath touched her neck, and he felt an answering pull in his body. He wanted to press his lips to that spot, but it wasn't time yet. She had to make the first move, though he wasn't opposed to helping that decision along.

"It's messy," she said.

"It doesn't have to be."

"Says the man whose life isn't lived surrounded by very observant family members."

"I can be very sneaky when motivated." He took off his hat so he could lean closer to her neck, so his breath would be hot against her skin. "And I'm very motivated."

"Dammit." The word seemed torn from deep down inside of her as she turned to face him, and then she gathered the front of his shirt in her fist and hauled him toward her.

Hell, yeah.

Irish wasn't much of a romantic, but as his mouth finally claimed Mallory's, he thought of fireworks exploding against a night sky.

He dropped his hat without care to where it landed—something he'd never done before—so he could cup the back of her neck. Her skin was so soft, and so were her lips. *Gentle*, he thought. This woman was soft and sweet and he needed to be gentle.

But then his sweet, gentle woman made a low growling sound in her throat and threaded her fingers through his hair and he forgot to hold back. She was backed against the bar and he put his other hand on her waist as his tongue slid between her lips.

Mallory's fingers tightened in his hair and he pressed his body against hers as she moaned. She caught his bottom lip between her teeth and he sucked in a breath. One of her legs curled around his calf and his heart pounded as he poured everything he'd felt since the second he laid eyes on Mallory into the kiss. She arched her back as their tongues danced, and her breasts pressed against him.

Irish's mind whirled with a need to take her—up against the wall, down in the cellar, making a dash for his camper or wherever he could get his hands on her naked body—but he hit the mental brakes hard.

He wanted her to *choose* to make love with him. Maybe it was a distinction that didn't make sense and that he'd regret later, but he didn't want Mallory to simply allow herself to be swept up in the moment—to come to him with a muttered curse of surrender on her lips. He wanted her to make a deliberate decision to make the space in her life for them to be together.

Forcing himself to break off the kiss, he took a small step back, though he kept his hand on the back of her neck for a few more seconds. They were both breathless, and the only way he could summon the strength to resist kissing her again was to bend over and pick up his hat.

He slapped it against his thigh and then settled it back on his head before looking at her again. "When you're running through your *pros and cons of sleeping with Irish* list, maybe keep tonight in mind."

Her eyes narrowed, but he saw the corners of her mouth twitching as she fought a smile. "You don't play fair."

"No, ma'am." He winked at her and then very reluctantly turned to the open box on the bar. "Let's get this done."

Chapter Seven

It's ladies' night at Sutton's Place Brewery & Tavern! Women drink for half price all night, and just in time since the kids have next week off from school for spring break. Stonefield House of Pizza is offering twenty percent off any orders delivered to the tavern. As always, soda and coffee are free for designated drivers (men, it's your turn) so enjoy your girls' night out safely and responsibly!

—*Stonefield Gazette* Facebook Page

The men in their lives had made it very clear that the Sutton women weren't exempt from enjoying the first official ladies' night in Stonefield. They'd objected, of course, but Lane had put his foot down—the men would be doing all the work. Irish would be behind the bar and Lane and Case would handle everything else.

Mallory even managed to arrange for Jack and Eli to sleep over with friends, and as she looked at herself in the mirror, she realized that not only was it the first time she'd bothered with makeup in so long, it was probably expired and should be thrown away, but she couldn't even remember the last time she'd been free of all responsibility.

Her kids were off enjoying themselves with their friends, being watched over by families she trusted. The taproom and the nachos and the dirty glasses wouldn't be her problem tonight. And they wouldn't be her mother's problem, either. Or her sisters'.

Tonight was just for fun.

Of course, she couldn't think about fun without thinking about Irish because the prospect of fun between the sheets with him had been the sole topic of her conversations with herself for the last four days. That kiss had changed everything. It was one thing to fantasize about the possibilities of the unknown.

But now she *knew*.

Now she knew what his body felt like against hers and what his mouth felt like, and how the beard and mustache tickled. She knew how much she liked the way his rough hand cupped her neck. She knew she wanted to feel all of that again, but with no clothing between them.

Mostly, she knew the chemistry between them was as potent as she'd thought and not something her imagination had cooked up because it had been a while since she'd been with a man.

Not tonight, she reminded herself for the umpteenth time that day. She was going to relax with her mom and her sisters and Molly and, for once, get to enjoy the business they'd built together.

From the moment Lane unlocked the doors, the place was packed. He'd reserved the Sutton women seats at one of the long tables, thank goodness, but it was crowded and loud. The guys would have their work cut out for them tonight.

She told herself not to watch Irish work. It wouldn't take too many glances before the women in her life caught on to her interest and then they'd pounce. Especially once Molly arrived and joined them. Her best friend was too perceptive, by far.

A few looks passed between them, though. Irish might not be expressive, but she'd had no trouble seeing the appreciation on his face when she walked through the door. Not that she'd taken extra trouble with her appearance tonight for his sake, but…okay, maybe she had. As busy as he was, and as much as she was enjoying the women's company, she kept her eye on him. And because she was, she knew he was keeping his eye on her.

His interest made her feel wanted—desired—and she liked it.

"Mal, are you even listening?" Gwen said, yanking Mallory's attention away from the cowboy behind the bar.

"Absolutely," she said with a straight face. Gwen simply gave her that big-sister stare she was so good at until she cracked. "Fine. No, I wasn't listening."

Molly grinned. "What were you thinking about?"

"Nothing," she replied, giving her best friend a look that she hoped translated to *don't.* "What were you saying, Gwen?"

"Laura told Mom they should go on a cruise next summer and we're trying to talk her into it."

"Who knows if I'll be able to afford it?" her mom said, reminding them all that their father had sunk every penny they had—even Ellen's vacation fund—into opening the brewery.

"Look around," Mallory said, waving a hand in the direction of the full tables. "You'll be able to afford it."

They talked about cruises—Caribbean versus Alaskan versus some other place, even though none of them had ever taken one—until Ellen waved her hand. "I'll think about it, but let's talk about something else."

Mallory could tell that, as much as her mom liked the idea of going on a cruise with her best friend, the sorrow at not being able to enjoy a cruise with her husband would raise its head at odd times. She'd have to urge her mom to talk about it with her grief counselor, because an adventure with Laura would be fun and her mom deserved it.

And her mom had also decided on their next topic. "Gwen, how is the wedding planning going?"

"We're not having a big wedding, Mom."

"Then it shouldn't be hard to plan. At least pick a date."

"We're not in a rush," Gwen responded, more firmly. "We're happy right now, and we'll probably pick a date soon, but there's been a lot going on."

"Do I get to be maid of honor?" Evie asked, grinning at Gwen. "You know Mallory's going to be busy making sure everything goes smoothly, like an unpaid wedding planner."

"We haven't gotten that far yet," Gwen said, frowning at Evie.

Evie just rolled her eyes. "You know I'm right."

Mallory knew she was right, too. She'd be busy making sure everything went smoothly for Gwen and Case, and that was hard to do when you were standing next to the bride, holding her flowers. Molly, who had been Mallory's maid of honor, was an option because she'd been friends with both of them growing up, but she and Gwen hadn't been as close since Gwen moved away. Gwen's best friends from school had moved away years ago. Evie was probably the most logical choice, but there was often conflict between the oldest and youngest sisters, so it might circle back to Mallory juggling *all* the plates. But she didn't want any of that conflict seeping in tonight and she could see Gwen losing patience with Evie, so a quick change of subject was in order.

"What are we ordering from Stonefield House of Pizza?" she asked, too suddenly and too loudly, so they all turned to look at her. "Sorry. I'm starving."

They ended up sharing a pizza, which took forever to arrive. By the time they'd finished it off, they were all a little tipsy, but Evie wasn't done yet.

"Mal, go get more beer."

"More?" She wasn't sure she wanted another.

"I'm good," Gwen said, and her mother nodded to indicate she was, too. "With beer, I mean. I'm not ready to leave yet."

"Come on," Evie said, giving her one of the high-wattage grins nobody could resist. "We've worked so hard and we're having so much fun. And Irish isn't busy right now. It's the perfect time."

Perfect time for what? Rather than open the door to any more discussion about Irish, just in case that's what Evie was hinting at, she stood up. Yes, she was definitely tipsy, but they'd been working hard, dammit, and it was a girls' night out. She'd earned a few drinks.

Irish saw her coming and, without taking his eyes off of her, shifted to the empty end of the bar. The crowd was thinning as it got late, and he waited at a spot that was as private as possible in the taproom. His tips twitched when she leaned against the bar and smiled at him.

"I thought you'd all be done by now," he said, amusement heavy in his voice.

"I did, too, but Evie wants another one and she wants me to have one, too. Mom and Gwen are done, though."

"Same as before?" She didn't realize she'd made a face until he frowned. "No?"

Oops. She'd given herself away. Leaning forward across the bar, she crooked her finger to beckon him closer. "Can I tell you a secret?"

He didn't smile, but she saw the spark of interest in his eyes and in the subtle way he shifted toward her. "You can tell me *all* your secrets."

The way he said it made her shiver, and she had to admit it was tempting. Not that she really had many secrets worth sharing, but if she did, she wouldn't mind whispering them in his ear. She knew they'd be safe with him.

"I like Evie's beer more than mine," she said quietly, leaning in. Even though the bar was between them, they'd both leaned in enough so their heads were almost together. "It's better. Hers is fun and… perky. Dad made her a perky beer."

"It's different, but that doesn't mean it's better," he said, and she got the impression his response was bland on purpose. As though he didn't want to cast judgment on the way David Sutton had concocted brews to show how he felt about his daughters.

"Mine's boring," she continued. "I mean, it's good enough, I suppose. But it's not deep and rich like Gwen's, or perky like Evie's. It's just there, being steady and boring, like a mom. My dad brewed me a mom beer, Irish."

"I regret that I never got to meet your father because he must have been one hell of a guy, but I've spent some time with Lane talking about him, and he showed me that notebook your dad kept, and I don't think for a second he was trying to make you a steady, boring mom beer." He tilted his head a little, so she could really see his eyes under the brim of his hat. "Steady, maybe. But not boring. I think he wanted to express that you're the rock of the family, staying in town and bringing everybody together."

A sheen of moisture clouded her vision, but then his fingertips touched hers on the bar. The contact was nothing anybody in the taproom would notice, but she felt it like a shock through her body.

"And sweetheart," he said in that low, husky way that made every nerve ending in her body tingle, "anybody who thinks you're boring isn't paying attention."

In her mind, she scrambled over the top of the bar and threw herself into his arms. He'd catch her, of course, but her weight would stagger him. He'd brace himself against the wall and all of those glasses would shatter on the floor, but she wouldn't care. She wanted his hands on her. His mouth on her. She wanted to run her fingertips over every inch of his hard body.

In reality, though, she didn't move. They were both perfectly still, with their fingertips touching and their gazes locked. The voices in the taproom faded away until her entire world was the soft sounds of their breathing and Irish's eyes.

He might not be the most expressive man she'd ever met, but the heat and the intensity in those eyes spoke volumes. All she had to do was give him the signal and the torment would end. No more wondering what it would be like to be with him. What his hands would feel like on her skin, or the strength in those firm muscles… She could stop daydreaming—imagining what it would be like to be with him—when she should be focused on things like sleeping or making sure the potatoes didn't boil over.

"The boys are at sleepovers tonight," she said in a whisper and heat flared in his eyes.

Then he set his jaw a stubborn way and gave a brief shake of his head. "And you've been drinking."

"Not a lot."

"You've had enough so you're saying things out loud you normally wouldn't, so as soon as I'm done working this bar, I'm locking myself in my camper for the night. Alone." She grinned until he pulled his hand back and straightened. He wasn't teasing. "So you want me to pour you Evie's brew?"

The sudden distance between them—and the very temporary regret that she'd fallen for such a genuinely good guy he couldn't overlook a little alcohol—took her voice for a moment, until she cleared her throat. "No, I'll have mine. I don't want them to know I don't love mine."

"You know Gwen is drinking Evie's, right?"

"True, but Gwen's is a stout," Mallory countered and she shuddered at the thought of drinking it, while being thankful she didn't have to explain that drinking her own brew was the easiest way to not make any waves with her mother or sisters. "And she's not a big beer lover, either."

After giving her a raised-eyebrow look that made her feel as if he understood more than she would have liked, he set out Evie's refill and then poured her a glass of the wheat beer her father had brewed in her honor and slid it across the bar to her. He didn't pull his hand back right away, though, and their fingers touched again.

"Howdy, Irish," a woman said as she stepped up to the bar, and Mallory didn't even look to see who it was. She took her beer and after giving Irish a small smile, took her drink back to her table.

She'd settled into her seat and had a sip of the nice, bland beer before she realized her mom, her sisters and Molly were all staring at her. For a few seconds, she wondered if she'd dribbled beer or nacho cheese on her shirt, but then she realized the stares were speculative. And expectant. They'd all been watching her at the bar and they wanted to know what all *that* was about.

She had no intention of telling them the truth.

"Irish was just telling me how much beer he's poured tonight," she lied.

"You looked very close," her mom said.

"Well, it's very loud in here. Hard to hear."

"When I first looked, I thought you two were kissing," Molly said, and then she laughed as if to show how silly she'd been and guilt shot through Mallory.

She hadn't told her best friend that she'd kissed Irish. It wasn't a matter of trust. Even though Molly was close to the entire family and wasn't known for having the best verbal filter, Mallory knew if she asked Molly to keep a secret, she wouldn't tell a soul. But she knew if she told her, Molly would feel it was her best-friend duty to urge Mallory to have a hot, sexy fling with the cowboy.

And Molly wouldn't be wrong. Mallory deserved to grab some pleasure if she wanted it. But, even though they'd been in each other's lives since toddlerhood and seen each other's ups and downs, Molly couldn't understand how hard it had been when Mallory had finally thrown Jeff out of the house. She didn't have to help Jack and Eli navigate the disentangling of an almost-blended family when she finally realized fellow single-parent Lewis wasn't really in love with her. And then had come the grieving for their beloved grandpa.

Eventually she would casually date again. Maybe even find a guy who made her feel the way Irish did, though at this moment, that didn't seem likely. But she wouldn't introduce a man into Jack and Eli's world as a potential father figure again until she was sure it would stick for the long haul.

She couldn't casually date Irish. The man lived in their yard and everything they did, they'd do surrounded by her family. And there was no long haul. He'd blown into town and, even though he was staying longer than he'd originally intended, he was just there to brew beer with his old buddy and then he'd be hooking his truck to his house on wheels and going down the road.

Irish woke from a dream about Mallory, cursing the well-trained internal clock that had been getting him up before the crack of dawn since he was a small boy. It had just been getting good.

It wasn't the first dream he'd had about her—and it probably wouldn't be the last—but it had been the most vivid and he wished more than anything that he could force himself to go back to sleep and slide in right where he'd left off.

It had been four days since the ladies' night at the bar and while he'd barely seen Mallory, he hadn't thought about anything *but* her. He spent a lot of his time in the brewing cellar, keeping himself busy learning Lane's system and even taking over a lot of the tasks that needed doing. It kept him from having to come up with odd jobs to do in the yard just on the off chance he might catch a glimpse of her, but it gave him plenty of time to relive that kiss. And to imagine a thousand wicked other ways that kiss could have ended.

And mostly, he wished she'd been sober the night the boys slept over at friends' houses. It would have been the perfect night for her to sneak into his bed, and maybe having several beers made her worry less about what her family would think, but taking advantage of that wouldn't sit right with him.

He was exiting his camper after a short lunch break when he spotted Mallory walking across the driveway toward him. Luckily, he had a lifetime of hiding his emotions behind a bearded mask, so he didn't think she'd be able to read on his face that he'd spent the morning thinking about all the places on her body he'd like to put his mouth.

She looked slightly frazzled, but he knew the boys hadn't gone to school yesterday *or* today, so that could explain it. "I have a favor to ask, but you're free to say no if you're busy."

The words *I don't think I could ever say no to you* almost fell out of his mouth before he clenched his jaw and took a second. He'd basically told her no a few nights ago, and it also gave away too much. "I'm not busy."

"You should at least hear what the favor is first. Also, it's not really a favor for me, but for my mom. I'm involved, though."

That was enough for him, but he'd play along. "What's the favor?"

"We have a bench at the thrift shop—like a garden bench thing with box storage under the seat—and Mom has a customer who wants it, but she has no way to get it home. Case's truck is in the shop getting a recall done and Laura can't find her keys to Lane's truck. But it's not like it has to be delivered today, so it's okay if you don't want to."

He wasn't sure why she was so adamant he could opt out if he wanted. She was either really worried about imposing on his time or she had some concerns about being seen in town with him. It's not as if he was big into public displays of affection, so even if he wanted to, he wasn't going to haul her into his arms and kiss her in the middle of the street.

And besides the fact he wouldn't say no to Mallory, he also wasn't going to opt out of helping out Mrs. Sutton. "I'm ready whenever you are."

"Well, there's more to it." She sighed, but he just waited until she got to the point. "The boys have no school this week and I was going to sign them up for vacation camp, but with the thrift store and the taproom… I just wanted the time with them. It would be so much easier for me to show you how to get to where the bench needs to go, but I don't have anybody to watch Jack and Eli."

He didn't see the problem. "My truck has a back seat."

She chuckled. "Your truck's big enough to have a guest bedroom and a half bath of its own, but that doesn't mean you want two boys with school vacation energy in it."

"They don't bother me." He was actually getting used to their energy and their volume, and he liked watching them play. There was a little piece of his heart that was both hurt and healed at the same time by seeing that his own childhood hadn't had to be what it was, and that there should have been a hell of a lot more joy in it.

"Okay, I'll get them ready. Mom's going to watch the parking and put cones out to save some spots in front of the store. The bench isn't that heavy, but we don't really want to carry it down the street to wherever you manage to park that thing."

By the time they got into town, Mrs. Sutton had managed to save enough space for him to park, and it was almost in front of the store. Mallory got out to move the cones and then, once he'd killed the engine, she had both boys get out on the passenger side. They took off at their usual gallop and were entering the thrift shop by the time he got around the truck to the sidewalk, where Mallory was waiting for him.

A couple of women were walking toward them, and one lit up when she saw him. "Howdy, Irish!"

Gritting his teeth, he grasped the brim of his hat and gave it a little dip. "Howdy, ma'am."

It was utterly ridiculous, but judging by the sparkly smile and happy sigh as the women passed, he'd played his role well. Judging by the judgmental sniff from the woman at his side as they walked toward the thrift shop, however, not everybody was a fan.

"Maybe we should find you a piece of hay to chew on, so it can hang out of your mouth," Mallory said, and the peevishness in her voice amused him to no end.

"No." He wasn't putting hay in his mouth. "I think that's farming, not ranching."

"Like anybody would know the difference."

"I know the difference." He pulled open the door to the thrift shop and held it for her.

"Mom!" As soon as they stepped through the door, Jack was there to take Mallory's hand, tugging her toward the back of the store.

"Stop pulling at me, Jack. What is it?"

The kid stopped tugging, but didn't let go of her hand. Since Mrs. Sutton was talking to a customer and he had no idea where to find the bench that needed to be loaded into the back of his truck, Irish followed Mallory and the boys.

"This is just like Corey's!" Jack was pointing to a bicycle. "It's the same kind, but his is green with black and this one's black with green. They're like a pair and he's my best friend and wouldn't be it cool if we had matching bikes?"

"You have a perfectly good bike," she pointed out.

"It's getting too small for me and if you get me this bike, then Eli can have mine because his is getting too small for him."

"You don't need a new bike right now," she said sternly.

"But Moooooom, I—"

"Jack. I said no."

The boy looked like he was going to argue the point, and Irish watched the exchange silently. He never would have asked his old man for a bike, but if he had worked up the courage and then been told no, he wouldn't have dared argue.

"But my birthday is coming up real soon," the boy insisted.

"I already bought your birthday present and your bike is *not* too small for you. We're not spending money we don't have to just so you and Corey's colors can match. Mrs. Field just left, so go say hi to your grandmother and keep her company while Irish and I load up the bench."

Once the boys had walked away—Jack uncharacteristically slowly and with several mournful glances over his shoulder at the bike—Mallory shook her head. "I forgot this was here or I wouldn't have brought them in. He'll definitely outgrow his bike before next summer, but this one needs a lot of work. It wasn't taken care of and the brakes and the cables are shot, and one of the tires is flat. We just don't have the time for that, so I'm hoping to get him a new bike for Christmas. He won't really be able to ride it until spring and maybe it won't match his best friend's bike, but he'll have one."

Irish nodded and then followed her through the store to the garden bench with a Sold sign on it. It was more awkward than heavy, and it took longer to get the boys out of the toy section and back into the truck than it did to load the bench in the back.

The actual delivery took longer than he'd expected. Not because of the drive, which wasn't long despite being down a network of back roads, but because the bench's buyer had heard all about the new cowboy in town and had insisted on meeting him.

Once they were in his truck again and headed toward town, though, he realized he didn't want this outing to come to an end. He enjoyed the chatter of the two boys in the back seat, and he *really* liked having Mallory next to him.

"Is there any place in town to get ice cream?" he asked in such a low voice, Mallory had to lean closer to hear him.

"Ice cream!" both boys yelled before their mother had a chance to answer him.

He winced and held up a hand. "Sorry. I didn't think they'd hear me."

"If you'd mentioned cleaning their rooms, they wouldn't have heard you. But ice cream? You can't whisper that softly enough. And we do have a favorite ice cream shop if you're sure you're up to it."

Luckily the shop was on the outskirts of town, so he was able to pull his truck off the side of the road and didn't have to worry about finding a parking spot near the small wooden ice cream shack. It was the kind of place with one ordering window and one pick-up window, with a huge, wooden cartoon cow. The four of them gathered in front of the massive chalkboard sign that listed all of the flavors.

"What kind do you want, Irish?" Eli asked. "I want black raspberry with jimmies in a cone!"

Irish was confused. "Who's Jimmy?"

Eli laughed. "You're funny."

He looked at Mallory over the boy's head, trying to telegraph with his eyes that he needed help. She was trying not to laugh at him, and only partially succeeding.

"Chocolate sprinkles," she told him. "We call them jimmies in this part of the country."

"Why?" She shrugged and he shook his head. "You eat ham boiled in water with cabbage by choice, and you name ice cream toppings after people. I don't know about you folks."

"Don't forget our narrow, windy streets and tiny parking spaces."

His chuckle was like a low rumble in his chest,

and the muscles in his face twitched, as if they really wanted to grin at her. Mallory's eyebrow arched, as though she could tell he'd been on the verge of laughing out loud, but he was saved by the kids.

"Mom!" Jack said impatiently, while Eli tugged at her hand.

Her gaze lingered on Irish's mouth for a few more seconds before she gave her sons her full attention. "Yes, ice cream. But we're in Irish's truck, so you're not getting cones. Order it in a dish."

"We're not eating *in* the truck," Jack pointed out, and it struck Irish again how comfortable they were pushing back against their mother.

They weren't disrespectful. It wasn't exactly back talk. But neither of them were afraid to argue a point with Mallory, and he was starting to grow accustomed to it. Kids had never really been a part of his life, so he only had his own childhood to go by. If he'd so much as thrown his father a look that could be taken as questioning the old man, he would have been black and blue.

Sometimes he'd wondered what kind of father he would be. Not that he'd seen it happening in his future because he'd never really had anything to offer a woman and that was okay with him. He'd always been afraid he would revert to the only manner of raising a child he'd known. But the more time he spent around Jack and Eli, the more he was able to see that whatever demons had driven his old man weren't waiting to rise up in himself.

Raising kids was maybe like breaking a horse, he thought. You didn't want to break the horse's spirit. Rules, boundaries, mutual respect. In the case of the Sutton boys, a lot of unconditional love. Irish's father had tried to break his spirit, but he hadn't succeeded.

"You both wear your ice cream as much as eat it," Mallory was saying. "And last time Aunt Gwen took you for ice cream, her seats were sticky and covered with smeared jimmies. You'll get dishes and wash up before you get in Irish's truck."

He was tempted to tell her it didn't matter—that kids making the truck seats sticky wasn't the kind of thing that would bother him—but she was using her mom voice and he didn't want to undermine her. Instead, he watched as they ordered their ice creams and added his own dish of peach ice cream—with jimmies, of course, because the boys liked them—to the list. The dishes came out in order and he'd made it clear he was paying, since he'd invited them, so Mallory and the boys took theirs and went to claim a picnic table.

As he dropped his change in the tip jar and picked up his ice cream, he watched Jack and Eli run ahead of Mallory. Even though he saw her gesture at them and heard her say something he couldn't quite make out, they sat on the same bench, leaving their mother—and Irish—to sit across from them.

He really did like those boys.

They'd also chosen one of the smaller picnic tables, so Mallory leaned out of the way while Irish stepped over the bench to sit. Once he was settled, he watched the boys inhaling their ice cream for a few seconds before digging into his own.

There wasn't a lot of room under the table, so it was inevitable that his leg brushed against Mallory's. He stilled for a few seconds and when she didn't pull away, he relaxed. Above the table, they looked like two very platonic friends taking the kids out for ice cream.

But under the table? Irish savored the warm pressure of her leg against his, and thought about that kiss. He thought about that kiss a *lot*, and he was surprised they weren't putting out enough heat just being this close together to melt all the ice cream they were eating. He shifted his boot in the grass, causing his leg to slide against hers, and he heard her wistful sigh.

He could wait. He was a patient man. Especially if waiting meant more days like today. While he wouldn't mind some alone time with her, spending time with her and her sons was a pleasure in itself. He enjoyed the way Jack and Eli would talk about anything and everything, always making sure Irish was a part of their conversations. And Mallory's expression when she was trying to be stern with them but was on the verge of laughing at their antics was fast becoming one of his favorite things.

Maybe it was a risk, allowing himself to feel like he belonged in this moment with them, but he knew it was worth it.

Chapter Eight

To the mom in the red Ford Escape who pulled into the elementary school drop-off line early on Monday morning to find nobody else there because it's school vacation week: trust me, we've all been there. Chelsea Grey, owner of the Perkin' Up Café, is offering one free caffeinated beverage to all moms this week!

—*Stonefield Gazette* Facebook Page

By the end of school vacation, Mallory was exhausted. Jack and Eli had been running her ragged during the day. And thinking about Irish was costing her sleep at night.

She needed for her sons to go back to school. And she very, very much needed to kiss Irish again. And again and again.

He was waiting for her to take the initiative, and she appreciated that. She liked that he respected her boundaries and had a solid grasp on consent, but there was a part of her that wished he would just sweep her off her feet. Literally. Take worrying about making a decision out of her hands by throwing her over his shoulder and tossing her onto his bed.

She knew he'd gladly do that, but not until she told him it was okay if he did.

"Are you burning the bacon?"

Startled by Evie's voice, Mallory blinked and realized she was, in fact, in danger of burning the bacon and that would be a tragedy. It was the best part of Sunday breakfast, since they usually stuck to the basics during the week.

Then she heard her mother yelling out the back door. "Irish, come in here and get some breakfast!"

As always when it came to that man, half of Mallory hoped he'd accept the invitation and she'd get to sit across the table from him and enjoy his company, while the other half hoped he'd decline and she wouldn't have to sit across the table from him, wishing they were alone.

Truthfully, though, it wasn't really half and half. Seventy-thirty maybe. She definitely wanted to see him, even if it was torture.

"I don't want to impose, Mrs. Sutton," she heard him say, which meant he was right outside.

"You already know my response to that, so come inside. Evie kept Mallory from burning the bacon, and I just finished scrambling a batch of eggs. I also made blueberry muffins last night and they're very good, if I do say so myself."

"You know I can't resist a good blueberry muffin."

Mallory turned in time to see him sweeping off his hat as he crossed the threshold into the kitchen, and her heart—along with other parts of her body—did a little happy dance at the sight of him. And when he ran his hand through his hair, as he always did when he took off his hat, her knees got so weak she was afraid she'd collapse and drop the well-done bacon.

"Good morning, boys," he said to Jack and Eli, who had just finished setting the table.

They were happy to see him and told him all about the video game their grandmother had brought home from the thrift store for them. And even though she wasn't sure the man had ever played a video game, he listened and asked all the right questions to keep them going until they were all seated.

Jack and Eli wanted to sit on either side of Irish, so Mallory ended up across from him, which was going to make it hard to avoid eye contact. But as long as she didn't let her mind wander too much, she'd be okay. Probably.

Dishes were passed and conversation fell by the wayside as everybody dug into their breakfast. Ellen liked to have the family together on Sunday mornings. Sometimes Gwen and Case joined them, but more often than not, they didn't. Because Case left for work so early in the morning during the week, Gwen liked to have lazy weekend mornings, and Mallory didn't blame her. She'd like to have a lazy weekend morning, too.

"Do you know what haiku is, Irish?" Jack asked, and Mallory sighed because he hadn't quite swallowed the bacon he was chewing yet.

"Poetry, isn't it? The one with the syllables?"

Jack nodded. "We're learning about them in school, and we had to write two over vacation."

The way he made it sound as if the teacher had assigned him some cruel and grueling punishment made her smile. "I remember doing that when I was about your age. And if I remember correctly, your aunt Gwen filled a whole notebook with them."

They all laughed, and Ellen nodded. "She was obsessed with them, and she made me read every single one she wrote."

"At least she was good at it," Evie pointed out. "I was not."

Ellen chuckled. "Poetry is not one of your strong

suits. But Jack, you go back to school tomorrow. Did you write yours yet?"

He nodded, and when they all just looked at him—waiting to hear it—he rolled his eyes.

"Pizza, round and hot.
I hide the crusts in the box.
Extra cheese is best."

Of course he'd written about pizza, Mallory thought. It was his favorite thing. "Aren't they supposed to be about nature?"

"Pizza is food and food is part of nature," her son said.

"Pizza? Really?" Mallory laughed.

"Tomatoes," Irish said, meeting her eyes across the table. "Wheat. Cheese. All very natural things."

"See?" Jack sat up straighter in his chair, excited to have an ally. "Irish says pizza is nature!"

"Oh well, if Irish says." Mallory shook her head, but she couldn't help laughing with the rest of the family, especially when she caught the amused glimmer in Irish's eyes. "You said you have to write two. What's the other one?"

"Boomer's poo is brown.
Stinking up Case's backyard.
Steaming in winter."

consider the hours right now, though. "We'll be back. Boys, you'll come, too. You can run around with Joey and if I buy anything, you can pull the wagons."

Mallory kept her eyes on her plate as a sizzling sensation swept over her body. Her mother was leaving and taking Evie and the boys with her. She and Irish would be alone. And at this point, she didn't even care that her mom was probably matchmaking and had planned the outing deliberately. Now that she'd remembered the clock was ticking when it came to Irish, she didn't want to waste any more time.

Thirty minutes later, Mallory was alone in the house. And, as far as she was concerned, that was a problem. Irish was supposed to be here with her. But another fifteen minutes passed without him knocking on her door, and she was starting to wonder if he'd missed the significance of what was happening here.

But then she thought about the way he didn't push. He let her know he wanted her, but he wasn't aggressive about it, and there was a good chance the only way they were going to take advantage of this brief respite from her ever-present family was if she went to him.

When she opened the back door, intending to go find him, she found him sitting on the bottom step. He had his hat in his hands, turning it around and

around by the brim, and he looked over his shoulder at her when the door opened.

"How long have you been sitting here?" she asked as he pushed himself to his feet.

"Just waiting until you make up your mind if you're going to invite me in or not."

"I was waiting for you to show up."

He tilted his head. "I couldn't know for sure."

She stepped back and swept her arm in a dramatic arc as she bowed slightly. "Consider yourself invited in."

He barely had time to toss his hat on the end of the counter and kick the door closed before she had him backed against it, stretching up on her toes to kiss him. He kissed her back with a hunger that matched her own, and her body melted against his.

He devoured her mouth and she buried one hand in his hair while the other grabbed the front of his shirt as though to hold him there. Not that he gave any indication he'd want to escape, but she couldn't help holding on to him as his tongue skimmed over hers.

When he moaned against her lips, his hand sliding over the curve of her ass before digging his fingertips into the soft flesh, heat flooded her veins and her fingers tightened in his hair. He shifted his leg, and the hardness of his thigh slipped between hers. With the hand on her ass, he yanked her forward so, even with two layers of denim between them, the friction made her gasp.

They needed to get out of the kitchen and up to her bedroom, she thought. And maybe he was thinking the same thing because his mouth left hers, traveling down her jaw and neck before he straightened his head so she could see his eyes.

"I'm done trying to resist you," she said breathlessly, her hand still fisted in his shirt.

"This was you resisting me?" He arched an eyebrow at her. "If so then, by all means, please keep resisting."

"No, that was me losing the last of my will to even try. I don't know where or when, but I'm going to get you in a bed." She smiled and released his shirt, running her hands down his chest to smooth the fabric. And to appreciate the wall of muscle under it, of course. "I don't know why I tried so hard in the first place."

"I know the list of reasons you gave me, but I don't feel like it's in my best interest to remind you of them right now."

"No, I remember them. But I also remember what I said that first weekend you were here, about being able to be all the things I am and still have sex if I want to. Just…sneaky sex, like you said."

"I can be sneaky."

"It's just… I mean it's not just about my family getting ideas. It's mostly the boys. They were so little when their father left, they don't really remember him, but they know he left. And they were pretty attached to Lewis—a single dad I dated—and his kids before that ended. And they were super close with my dad." Her throat worked as she swallowed past the sudden lump of emotion. "I can't keep you separate from them because they like you a lot, but I know you're leaving and I don't want the attachment to…grow in that way. I don't want them to have expectations that you're more than a fun family friend camping in the yard for a little while."

Something flickered across his face—an emotion he almost expressed, but that she couldn't quite catch—and then he nodded. "I get it."

"Good. Now let's get back to me not resisting you."

When Irish moved to kiss her, but then stopped, tilting his head, Mallory heard the footsteps in the hallway. And the low humming of an old song she couldn't stand. "Crap, it's Gwen."

She practically sprinted to the other side of the kitchen, grabbing a glass off the counter as if she was going to wash it or fill it or something. When she saw Irish's eyebrow arch, she realized she might have offended him with her desperation to not be seen touching him, but she couldn't do anything about it right now because her sister walked into the kitchen and stopped abruptly.

"Hi," Gwen said, her gaze bouncing between Mallory and Irish. "I...should I come back later?"

"No," Mallory said, too quickly. "What's up?"

Gwen's gaze darted away and there was a telltale blush of color on her cheeks. "I thought you all left together, so... I didn't think anybody was here."

"And you what? Just wanted to hang out alone in the kitchen?"

"I need to borrow the juicer."

Mallory gasped and pointed at her. "You were going to steal Mom's juicer?"

"Borrow, Mal. I need to borrow it."

"Borrowing is when you knock on the door and ask the owner if you can use it temporarily. Stealing is when you break in when you know nobody's home and take it."

Gwen laughed. "I didn't *break in.* And I was going to see if there's one in the shop room."

They often raided the tiny room, or oversize closet—they still weren't sure what its original purpose had been—because their mom stashed items meant for the thrift store in there. "You know Mom would never hold on to a juicer. They sell fast."

"I know." Gwen blew out a breath. "There isn't one for sale in this entire town."

"So order one online. You're not taking ours."

"Fine." She gave Irish a speculative look that made Mallory's stomach tighten. Was her sister going to get payback by embarrassing her? "You don't have a juicer in that camper, do you?"

"No, ma'am." His eyes crinkled. "There wasn't room for it, so I had to leave it behind in Montana."

Both sisters laughed, and then Gwen threw up her hands in surrender. "Fine. I'll order one online."

Mallory nodded. "And when you don't use it because it's easier to just buy juice at the market, feel free to donate it to the thrift shop."

"I'll use it, Mallory. I'm going to make *so* much juice." She waved a hand and spun on her heel to leave. "Bye, Irish. Good to see you."

He tipped his hat. "Ma'am."

Once Gwen was gone, Mallory looked at the clock and sighed. She had no idea how long the rest of the family would be gone, but with the clock ticking down toward opening the taproom for the night, she suspected it wouldn't be long. Especially since Evie was with them. She'd have fun looking at the flowers and taking pictures, but her enjoyment would be short-lived and then she'd want to move on to the next thing. That was just how Evie rolled.

"You think they'll be back soon?"

She held up her hands to signal that she had no idea. "It might be another hour, or it might be ten minutes."

As he looked into her eyes, obviously waiting for her to decide what came next, her body ached with the need to feel his hands again. But the possibility her children and her mother might walk through the front door at any time definitely put a damper on the mood. Especially after her sister almost walked in on them.

"I don't want to be listening for a car in the driveway," she said, her voice heavy with regret. Then she gathered her hands into fists and growled her frustration. "You must be so aggravated with this…with me."

She'd barely gotten the words out before her chin was caught in his gentle grip, and he tilted her head up so she could see the sincerity in his eyes. "I'm not aggravated with you. Waiting just makes a person appreciate things more."

"Really?" she asked, a little sarcastically because waiting was *killing* her.

"Yeah, really. If somebody randomly hands you a slice of apple pie, you eat it and okay, it was good apple pie. But if you just keep thinking about apple pie and you want it so badly—if you're really *craving* apple pie—and then you get a slice, it's the best damn apple pie you've ever had."

"Oh." The word came out so breathy it was more of a sound than an actual word.

"I'm really craving you, Mallory." He let go of her chin to run his thumb across her bottom lip. "And every ache and every sleepless night and every time I close my eyes and see your face will only make it all the sweeter."

Then, before she could gather enough coherent

thought to come up with a response, he kissed her forehead and walked out the back door. She wanted to run after him and…just grab him. Maybe tackle him to the ground and have her way with him right there in the yard.

Mallory snorted, amused at herself. Wouldn't Stonefield love *that*? Instead, she took a deep breath and tried to focus on what she should do with the rest of her free time, since she wouldn't be spending it kissing Irish. Or anything else with Irish, other than thinking about him and his apple pie analogy.

She decided a cold shower might be the best place to start.

"Are you even listening to me?"

"Are you saying anything worth listening to?"

Irish looked from Lane to Evie and back to Lane before taking a few steps back into the shadows. He wished he was anywhere else but trapped in the brewing cellar with these two at the moment. And maybe *trapped* was a strong word, since he could get out if he wanted to, but they were holding their verbal standoff between him and the stairs and there was no way to exit without it being awkward.

Even more awkward than listening to two exes snipe at each other.

"I don't like people down here. It's a delicate process."

Evie snorted. "No, you don't like *women* down

here. Irish is down here all the time. Case comes down here."

"They're helping me."

"This isn't your personal man cave, Lane Thompson." Evie pointed her finger and for a second, Irish thought she was actually going to poke Lane's chest. "This is my mother's business. This is my mother's carriage house and this is my mother's cellar."

"It's also *my* business, except for the actual building," Lane pointed out.

"Yes, because my dad thought going into business with my ex-husband was a supergreat idea. It doesn't change the fact that if I want to have a look around and check on my mother's investment, I'm going to do that."

Irish didn't like the way Evie's sunny disposition disappeared behind a dark, cranky cloud every time she was around Lane. It had been getting worse lately instead of better, and he was starting to wonder if something had happened between them. He wasn't going to ask because it was none of his business, but he liked them both and he didn't like seeing the friction between them.

"So you checked on it," Lane snapped. "Do you even know what you're looking at? Do you know what any of the tanks or gauges or lines are for? No. So you've seen it. And now we have sparging to take care of. Feel free to watch."

Evie spun on her heel and stormed up the stairs,

and Irish had no doubt if the glass door at the top was able to be slammed, she would have smashed the entire wall into glittering shards.

He worked alongside Lane, rinsing the mash grains, keeping his mouth shut. If his friend wanted to talk, he would. It wasn't in his nature to pry to begin with, but throwing in the fact Lane was his friend and Evie was Mallory's sister meant he wanted no part of this family drama.

Then Lane stopped, his hands braced against a tank and his head lowered. "Why, of all the women in the world, do I have to love that one?"

Irish's eyebrows shot up. That was new information. He knew Lane had loved Evie, of course. They'd been married. And back when they'd first met at the bar in Montana, Lane had talked about his girl back home and how he was going to marry her as soon as he had his degree. But that had been a long time ago, and he didn't realize Lane's feelings hadn't changed.

"I don't think we get to choose who we love," Irish said. He didn't know a damn thing about love, actually, but he had to say something.

Lane lifted his head and gave it a little shake. "One of the reasons I did the deep dive into brewing with David was just trying to fill the empty hours of the day because I learned a long time ago that Evie is not replaceable in my life. And now here we are."

"It seems to be getting worse between you," Irish said, since it was the truth.

"Yeah, probably because we had sex last week."

If Irish actually had a variety of facial expressions, he'd be pulling out the cartoon jaw-drop in that moment. He hadn't seen that coming. And how could two people who couldn't stand to be in the same room with each other for five minutes have sex in this place, but he and Mallory couldn't find a way to make it work? That wasn't fair at all.

"My mom had something for Ellen, and Evie stopped by the house to get it. It must have been Wednesday because the taproom wasn't open. My mom wasn't there. I was."

"It doesn't look like it helped a reconciliation along."

Lane snorted. "Reconciliation's never going to happen. Loving each other and great sex were never the problem. She left me because she didn't want to be tied down, and I had my dad's business to run and my mom to take care of. She still doesn't want to be tied down, and I still have a business to run."

Irish had run out of things to say, so he figured the best thing to do was simply listen. But Lane just shook his head again and then took a deep breath, like he could somehow cleanse himself of loving Evie.

"I hope you'll keep this between us," Lane said. "Case knows, but I know he won't tell Gwen. And I don't know if Evie will tell her sisters or not, but that's her choice. I'd rather they not find out. Or Ellen. I really hope it doesn't get back to Ellen."

"They won't hear it from me."

"Thanks." He pulled a couple of folding metal chairs from a corner of the room and popped them open. "Have a seat. I want to talk to you about something and these cement floors are hell on my back."

He wanted to talk *more?* Irish was feeling talked out, but he sat because he wanted to know what Lane had to say. And he wasn't wrong about the cement floors.

"I think you should brew up a special edition for the taproom," Lane said once they were seated, and that piqued Irish's interest. He'd much rather talk about brewing beer than relationships. "After all these years of talking about it, you must have something you'd like to try."

"I guess I didn't think too specifically, since I didn't think brewing with a real setup was something I'd ever do."

"Come on. You drove all this way and I have plenty of the house lager kegged, so now's your chance."

An image of Mallory laughing popped into Irish's head, and he couldn't help thinking of the bland beer that David Sutton had concocted for his middle daughter. He didn't want to disrespect the man, especially since that was probably how most of the family saw Mallory. He hadn't been here very long, but he could already see that she was the peacemaker and the mediator—the one who could get along with everyone, no matter what was going on.

He wouldn't mind taking a shot at brewing something that captured the Mallory *he* saw, and it wouldn't be bland. It would be vibrant as hell.

"Even if I do an ale, we're looking at a month," he said.

Lane shrugged. "You got somewhere to be?"

Nobody was expecting him anywhere, but he wasn't sure how Mrs. Sutton would feel about having his camper in her driveway for that long. Or how Mallory would feel about it. He knew her interest in him was based on the fact he'd be leaving town.

"We have enough equipment to mix it up once in a while," Lane continued. "The house lager is a staple, obviously, and we've had the three brews for David's daughters, but the way to keep people coming back is to keep giving them something new. And our customers have really connected with you behind the bar. I think they'd line up to see what you come up with."

"I'd like to give it a shot," Irish admitted.

Before Lane could say more, they heard the faint beeps of Evie's birthday being punched into the digital lock and then the thump of footsteps on the stairs. Too heavy to be a woman, Irish thought with relief. Though he had no problem with women in the cellar, he didn't want to witness another round of verbal sparring between Lane and Evie.

It was Case and when he saw them sitting, he pulled out another chair and made himself as comfortable as one could get on a folding piece of metal. "So, Irish, Gwen told me you foiled her plan to borrow Ellen's juicer—and I use the term *borrow* very loosely—yesterday morning."

Irish's muscles tightened slightly, though there was nothing in Case's tone to signal this conversation was going to go in an unpleasant direction. He prepared himself for being grilled about why he was alone in the house with Mallory. "Technically, it was Mallory who foiled her plan. I would have let her take it."

When Case chuckled, some of Irish's tension eased. "There isn't a single juicer for sale in this town. I told her to order one online but, as you may have noticed, the Sutton women can be stubborn."

Lane cocked his head. "To be fair, you did choose the most stubborn of them."

"That I did."

"Mrs. Sutton's no slouch in the stubbornness department," Irish pointed out, and both men laughed.

"Very true, though she can't get you to call her Ellen." Case grinned. "How come you call the women *ma'am* but don't call me *sir*?"

Irish gave him a look that would have made a lesser man piss himself. Case just laughed at him.

"I want to hear more about how the plan was foiled, though," Lane said, and Irish knew what he was really saying. He wanted to know about Irish and Mallory being alone in the house together.

"Well," Irish said, his tone dry. "Gwen thought everybody was gone and tried to sneak in and take the juicer. Mallory said she couldn't have it. The plan was foiled."

"For the love of pale ale," Case said. "We want to know what you were up to with Mallory."

If there was one thing Irish absolutely wasn't going to do, it was share Mallory's secrets with these two men. Or anybody. She'd made it very clear she didn't want her family to know about them, and they were close enough to family to count. So he just raised his eyebrow and looked Lane in the eye, and then Case, saying nothing.

To their credit, neither man squirmed. Most would have. Either he was losing his touch, or they weren't afraid of him. Probably a little of both, he thought.

"Look," Case said. "We like you. If we didn't, you wouldn't still be here. But Mallory…she's had a rough go and we're like her brothers."

"I actually *was* her brother-in-law once," Lane reminded Case. "But you can't be like her brother. That would be weird."

He rolled his eyes at Lane before turning to Irish. "Mallory and I dated in high school. We were kids. It's a long story, but not really a big deal."

Irish made a hmm sound and nodded. He hadn't known that, but it couldn't have been too big a deal since Gwen was going to marry him. And he certainly didn't care who Mallory had dated in high school. All he cared about was that she wasn't dating anybody else *now.*

Or ever again, really, but at some point in the future, it wasn't going to be his business anymore. She wanted fun? He'd give her fun. But what she didn't want from him was long-term.

"Back to what's actually relevant," Case continued, giving Lane a look. "We care about Mallory a lot and while we know she's a grown woman and what she does is none of our business, we can't help but keep an eye out for her, you know?"

He'd think less of them if they didn't.

"Ellen likes you, too," Lane added. "Hell, everybody does. So they might get ideas, if you know what I mean."

He did know what Lane meant. It would be hard not to, since not giving her family ideas was so high on Mallory's priority list, they were both suffering for it.

"You're not going to give us anything, are you?" Case asked.

Irish tilted his head slightly. "I guess if there's something Mallory wants you to know, she'll probably tell you about it."

"Dammit." Case leaned back in the chair and

folded his arms. "I admire that about you, Irish. I really do. But us guys, we help each other navigate the Sutton women, you know?"

"I don't need to navigate. Mallory's in the driver's seat and I'm just along for the ride."

"Just know we're in the back seat," Lane said, "watching you."

Case barked out a laugh. "You made it creepy, man."

"Yeah, that didn't come out right at all."

Amusement made Irish shake his head. The family and business dynamics might be messy, but Lane and Case were good guys. If he was sticking around, he knew they'd both be really good friends to him, probably for life.

But he wasn't sticking around. He might have extended his stay for a few more weeks, but he'd leave eventually. Not yet, though, so as they turned the conversation toward family stuff, Irish tuned them out and started sifting through the mental notes on brewing that he'd been compiling for years. He was going to take advantage of Lane's offer and brew up one hell of a special edition for Sutton's Place Brewery & Tavern.

For Mallory.

Chapter Nine

The hardware store accidentally ordered a massive surplus of tomato cages, so they're having a buy one tomato cage, get a tomato cage free sale! But according to Jerry, they have so many tomato cages that it's more like a buy one of anything and he'll give you a tomato cage. It's a great time to give those droopy tomato plants a boost!

—*Stonefield Gazette* Facebook Page

Mallory looked at the cast-iron contraption that Mrs. Eastman had set on the counter with an air of satisfaction—maybe even victory—that made no sense at all to her. "What is it?"

"It's an antique."

"I can see that. But an antique *what*, exactly?"

"I swear, you kids nowadays." Mrs. Eastman shook her head as if all hope was lost. "It's an apple peeler. You clamp it on the table, stick the apple here, and then crank the handle. It peels and cores the apple. It's a bargain right now, since it'll be in high demand come apple-picking season."

"Ah." It didn't seem like the kind of thing anybody would use anymore, but she supposed it was a novelty. And an antique, apparently. "Are you looking to sell it or place it on consignment?"

"I want to sell it." Mrs. Eastman pointed a finger at her. "And I don't want that sister of yours using it in a book, either."

Keeping the polite expression on her face wasn't easy for Mallory, because this sort of thing was why Gwen had moved away and lived in Vermont for so long. Many of the locals were convinced that Gwen's book, *A Quaking of Aspens*—which had been a breakout bestseller and then made into a movie which won a bunch of awards—was really about Stonefield, in the manner of *Peyton Place*. Years ago, Mrs. Eastman had donated a vase with hand-painted violets on it to the thrift shop, and there had been a vase with violets in *A Quaking of Aspens*. Mrs. Eastman hadn't been shy with her opinion of Gwen Sutton stealing their very lives for her books.

While Mallory couldn't deny a vase Gwen had

seen in her youth may have been something her subconscious had coughed up when she needed a detail for her book, she thought *stealing their very lives* was a bit much.

"I'll have to research the value before I can make an offer," she said.

Mrs. Eastman sniffed. "Ellen said she'd give me fifty dollars for it."

Mallory didn't believe for a second that the woman showing up during the two hours every Tuesday that her mother was out of town, seeing a grief counselor for the past few months, was a coincidence. She wasn't sure Mrs. Eastman knew where her mom was, but she knew she wouldn't be here.

"She'll be back in an hour if you'd like to stop back by," she said, not wanting to accuse Mrs. Eastman of anything, but also not about to hand over fifty dollars for an old gadget.

"I'm very busy today, though," Mrs. Eastman said, just as Mallory's phone chimed.

She glanced over to where it was propped against the register, and she was able to see that it was from Molly and read the preview.

Your cowboy bought condoms at the market.

"Oh no," she said aloud, and then realized the woman had still been talking. "I'm sorry, Mrs. Eastman, but this is an emergency. Now, you know I help out Mom here, but anything with a value over twenty dollars has to be handled by her. You're welcome to come back another time if you want to see her."

As expected, Mrs. Eastman took the twenty dollars and left, still grumbling about kids these days as the door swung closed behind her. As she tucked the apple peeler under the counter to price later, Mallory figured twenty dollars was at least ten dollars too many, but she didn't care. She had more important business to take care of.

Irish had bought condoms. At Dearborn's Market. She would have face-palmed, but her hands were busy unlocking her phone so she could call Molly.

"I guess you got my text," her best friend said in lieu of hello.

"We need a believable reason why he would buy a box of condoms that doesn't involve he and I having been seen out in town together."

"Like what? Balloon animals? Drug smuggling?" Molly paused for a few seconds. "There are probably a lot of things you can use condoms for, actually. I can make a list and—"

"Molly," Mallory said, before her friend went too far off on one of her tangents. "I meant we have to come up with somebody else he could be using them with, not starting a rumor he sits around making condom dachshunds."

"You can't do that, Mal."

She sighed. "I know."

"If it helps, only Donna and I know. I saw him checking out, but there was nobody in line with him."

"Donna Mack knowing is almost the same as the *Stonefield Gazette* putting it on their Facebook Page, you know." Mallory forced herself to take a deep breath in an effort to gain some perspective and calm down. She was a grown woman. She was single. It was nobody's business if she and Irish burned through an entire crate of condoms, and she wouldn't be doing anything wrong.

It was just the idea of everybody talking about it—and her family becoming invested in the outcome—that had her pacing tight circles behind the counter.

Before their lives had been turned upside down by her dad's death and having to get the brewery open, her mom and sisters had been increasingly pushy about wanting her to get out there and date again. Her mom hadn't exactly been subtle about putting Mallory in Irish's path with cold lemonade and bench deliveries. Condom buying could spin everything out of control.

"I know some stuff about Donna," Molly assured her. "She's not going to gossip about you and Irish."

Mallory wanted to ask what exactly Molly knew about Donna, but then she'd never get off the phone. And she was more focused on her own issues at the moment. "It's not like there's anything to gossip about. I feel like it's never going to happen, Molly.

There's always somebody around and I don't want it to become a big thing, you know? It's just...for fun."

"A fling!" Molly was so excited, one would think *she* was contemplating some no-strings-attached sex. "I could lend you a room, you know."

Mallory laughed so hard she had to wipe her eyes. "He can barely bring himself to park that massive truck in the funeral home parking lot. He's not going to have sex there."

"Trust me. I'm *very* aware of how many men don't want to have sex in a funeral home." She gave an exaggerated sigh. "But I know you're going to figure it out, Mal. It's meant to be."

Another customer arrived, so Mallory had to get off the phone, but she thought about that phrase—*it's meant to be*—and Irish buying condoms for the remainder of the day. Her mother even noticed her distraction when she returned to the store, but there was a zero percent chance Mallory wanted to confide in Ellen about her situation.

During her very short drive home, she lectured herself on how she should act when she saw Irish. No blushing. No dodging eye contact. Certainly no giggling. No climbing him like a bear cub climbing a tree.

She'd just gotten out of the car when the boys got home from school, so she greeted them at the sidewalk. As they walked into the house, she looked over her shoulder just in time to see Irish disappear into the carriage house. Lane's truck wasn't in the driveway. Case's truck wasn't across the street, so they were probably still on a job.

Irish was alone.

And Mallory was tired of doing this dance with him. *It's meant to be.*

"You boys sit at the table and do your homework," she told them. "I have to go out to the taproom for a few minutes, but I'll be right back. And I want to see the work you've done. I mean it."

Once they were settled, she walked out of the house and across the driveway before she could change her mind. She expected to find him in the cellar, but as soon as she walked through the door to the taproom, she saw him. He was standing on a stepladder, cleaning one of the long ceiling fan blades.

He looked down when he heard the door, and she liked the way his eyes lit up when he saw her. "How was work today?"

"Interesting," she said, admiring the way his jeans stretched over his behind as he backed down off the ladder.

"Mrs. Sutton mentioned there was dust gathering on the edge of the blades and I wasn't doing anything, so I figured I'd take care of it." He tossed the rag onto the stepladder and turned to face her. "So what was interesting about work?"

"Well, I got a news update this morning." She held up her phone so he could read the text from Molly.

Your cowboy bought condoms at the market.

He shook his head. “This town is too much.”

“Try growing up here.”

“*Your* cowboy, huh?”

She’d shown him the text before she remembered the phrasing Molly had used, but it was too late to take it back now. “I’ve been telling you all along my friends and family would get ideas.”

“Are you mad about this?”

She put her hands on her hips, giving him a fake stern look. “Did you buy them for us?”

He frowned. “I sure as hell didn’t buy them for anybody else.”

“Then I’m not mad about it.” She blew out a breath. “Now to figure out when we can actually use them.”

His eyes crinkled. “Finally. I was starting to think I was going to have to do something drastic.”

“What are you going to do, drop a rope around my shoulders and tie my ankles together?”

“Not really my thing, but I’ll try anything once if that’s what you’re into.” She felt her face flame, and he winked at her. “I was trying to come up with a plan that required me to drive to some town or city and getting your mom to volunteer you to ride with me so I don’t get lost, and then we could find a motel.”

She laughed. “That’s really not a bad plan.”

"I've been giving it a lot of thought. A *lot.*"

"Me too," she said. "Obviously my bed is out of the question because it's in my mother's house."

"You have two kids, so I'm pretty sure she knows you've had sex."

"Two kids who are *also* in the house. It's not so much a house rule as it is me not wanting to get you in my bed and then have a pillow over my face the whole time, worrying about being heard."

"Well, there's always *my* bed, you know."

She'd already considered and dismissed that option. "I don't think campers are all that soundproof."

"You're really worried about sound carrying. Are you planning to be that loud?"

She blushed and his eyes crinkled as if he was smiling without moving his mouth. "I'm not preplanning the decibel levels or anything, but my mother lives in that house and I won't be able to stop worrying about it being awkward."

"I'll hook the camper to the truck and drag it out in the middle of the woods somewhere."

"That would be discreet. *'Hey Mom. Irish and I are taking the camper out of here for an hour for no reason at all.'*"

He arched his eyebrow. "An hour?"

"Too long?" She gave him a saucy grin and shrugged. "Maybe we can stop for ice cream on the way back."

"If I ever figure out how to get you naked in my

bed—or *any* bed at this point—you're going to be there for longer than an hour and you won't have the strength to eat ice cream when I'm done with you."

"If you keep saying things like that, I'm not even going to have the strength to walk back to the house."

His eyebrow quirked up. "You could stay."

She wanted to. She really, really did. "I left the boys doing their homework, and I've already been out here long enough. I'll probably hear the scrambling to turn off a video game when I go inside."

"Not trying to be pushy," he said, "but I'd really like to have a plan before you walk away."

There was something incredibly sexy about the almost pleading tone in his husky voice. It was nice to be wanted so badly. "Leave your camper door unlocked when you go to bed tonight."

Their gazes locked and the air between them seemed to sizzle so hotly, she was surprised her clothes didn't burst into flames.

"Go be with your boys," he said finally. "I'll wait up for you."

Irish knew the hours between Mallory going back to the house and her sneaking into his camper were going to feel like the longest of his life, so the best thing he could do was keep himself busy.

He finished cleaning the ceiling fan blades and, since Lane hadn't shown up yet, he found other busywork. Then Mrs. Sutton needed a hand in the house, which he never minded doing. He didn't see Mallory while he was inside, but he could hear the low sound of her and the boys talking about something upstairs.

Finally, Lane showed up and they went down into the cellar.

"I didn't think we were ever going to finish to-day's job," Lane told him, obviously exhausted. "I'm so glad you're around, so I know everything's okay down here. I keep thinking one of the jobs—either the tree service or the taproom—will ease up, but I'm still running myself ragged."

"You know I'm happy to help out while I'm here." He wasn't making any promises about how long that would be because the only answer he could really give was *When Mallory gets tired of me and throws me in the toy box.*

"What smells like fruit?" Lane looked around, sniffing the air. "It smells like peaches or some-thing."

"Apricots," Irish muttered, because he knew Lane wouldn't let a strange odor in the cellar go unchecked.

"What smells like apricots?"

"My hands."

Lane turned away from the tank, giving Irish his full attention. "Why do your hands smell like apri-cots?"

"Mrs. Sutton asked me to change a light bulb in the hallway for her, so I was in the house. There was some hand cream in the bathroom, and I didn't realize it smelled like fruit until after I squeezed a bunch into my hand. Seemed a shame to waste it so now my hands smell like apricots."

"Apricot hand lotion." Lane snorted.

"My hands feel like rough-cut lumber." They probably had for years, but marveling at how small and soft Mallory's hand was in his for the last few weeks made him wonder if she'd noticed how tough and abrasive his were.

And that was just her hands. What would his hands feel like against the tender flesh of her breasts? The inside of her thighs?

In a few hours, if all went according to plan, Mallory was going to be in his bed and the last thing he wanted her thinking about was how rough his hands were. Smelling like apricots was a small price to pay as far as he was concerned.

Lane's phone chimed with the sound that signified it was one of the Sutton women and he sighed. "They must have seen my truck pull in. I love these women. Truly, I do. But there are times I think about how different it would be if David and I were running this show together and I really miss him."

Irish watched him read the text in silence, since there was nothing he could really say. He'd never met Mr. Sutton, obviously, so the only thing he knew about the man were things he'd been told. And that he'd been passionate about beer and about being a father, and he'd tried to bring those two things together.

Watching the three sisters together over the last few weeks had given him a better idea of why David Sutton had chosen the brews he had. Gwen had a strong personality, and Evie was lighter and more carefree. And Mallory was in the middle.

He'd been wrong about the wheat beer for Mallory. The brew Irish had planned for her would definitely not be bland. He was still mulling it over, thinking about which ingredients would give him the kick of flavor he was looking to get, but he'd bring his idea to Lane very soon.

Lane's sigh after he read the text was even more weary than when the phone had chimed. "Ellen wants to have a meeting and she wants everybody there, so she's making a big batch of spaghetti."

"At least your meetings come with food. That's not a bad gig."

"She specifically said to tell you that she expects you for spaghetti, too." Lane laughed at his scowl. "Yes, my friend. You get to sit through a Sutton's Place meeting. But hey, free spaghetti."

Irish was glad his friend had misread his reaction as not wanting to sit through a meeting about the brewery. Mostly he was worried about how hard it was for him to be in a room with Mallory and not give away that all he could think about was tonight finally being the night. Hopefully. He knew there was always a possibility something would come up—a family issue or a son who refused to go to sleep or something—but he was confident she'd do anything she could to be there.

"I'm not big on pasta, usually," he said.

Lane laughed. "You're not getting out of this, man. It's easier to just go along, but Ellen makes great sauce and Mallory's garlic bread is delicious. Worth listening to all of us talking."

There was a little commotion happening when they went inside because the dining arrangements had changed. With all of them together it was too tight a fit around the kitchen table, so they'd picked up the jigsaw puzzle pieces scattered around the dining room table and were in the process of moving all the place settings in there.

Irish didn't mind at all since he got seated next to Mallory.

The meeting part of the meal turned out to be nothing more than Mrs. Sutton wanting to talk about the storage area above the taproom.

"When we converted the carriage house, we didn't bother with the upstairs space because we had enough on our plates," she said once they'd all served themselves. "But now it's been a catchall for everything for almost a year, and it's getting out of hand."

"It's good for storage, though," Evie pointed out. "If not upstairs, where will we store everything?"

"You mentioned making it an office," Gwen

added. "But as Evie said, where would we keep all the stuff that's up there?"

"Not in the grain room," Lane said. "And definitely not in the cellar, either."

"Nobody suggested that, Lane," Evie said in a tone that was very different from the one she used with her sisters.

"We do need it for storage," Ellen agreed before the conversation could go south. "But we need to organize it and have a system for it. Do you know how many napkins we have? We keep buying them because we don't realize we already have plenty in the horror show pile of boxes upstairs."

"An inventory system on the computer would help," Evie said.

"Are you volunteering to set it up?" Gwen asked, her voice heavy with skepticism. "And that only helps if everybody updates it every time they open a package of napkins or a box of sanitizer or whatever it is."

"We can look into that," Ellen said, holding up her hand. "But let's start with a strategy for cleaning up and organizing what we already have."

The talk turned to various shelving options, but Irish didn't pay much attention. He was surprised Mallory hadn't said anything yet, since she usually ended up being the mediator during these kinds of discussions. But she seemed to be content to eat her pasta, twirling it onto her fork while her leg rested against his.

He wasn't sure about the spaghetti, but being able to sit next to Mallory with their bodies touching under the table made sitting through the meeting worthwhile. Especially since it was less a meeting than the family debating on wire versus wooden shelving. The tension between Lane and Evie was almost palpable, though, and more than once he'd watched Mrs. Sutton look from one to the other with a worried look on her face.

Once the meal was finished, Irish helped clean up and he didn't mind when Mrs. Sutton thrust a cloth and a bottle of wood cleaner in his hand and assigned him to washing the table. He'd used the cleaner before, and he really liked the warm almond scent. It would probably go nicely with the apricot hand lotion.

And now he was a guy who noticed how scents complemented each other, he thought with amusement as he polished the wood. If only the guys in the bunkhouse could see him now.

He'd just finished when Mallory appeared in the doorway to the dining room. After a final look to make sure nobody else was there, she stepped inside. There was no door, but Mrs. Sutton had told him once that the biggest drawback to the old New England houses was that they were the opposite of open concept. Small rooms with lots of walls and doorways.

"I'm sorry you had to suffer through that," she said in a quiet voice.

"I'm not. I like your family, and Lane wasn't lying about your garlic bread."

The compliment made her blush. "I'm glad you like it. And that you were able to get some since it's one of my boys' favorite meals if you don't count pizza."

"I noticed they really put it away tonight."

She tapped her temple with the tip of her index finger. "I let them fill up on carbs so they're a lot right now, but later they're going to crash hard and face-plant in their beds."

"A woman with a plan. I like it."

"Just so you know, part of the plan has to be me telling Evie I'm sneaking out. I can't leave the house without telling somebody where I'll be."

"Makes sense." The last thing he wanted was Mrs. Sutton panicking because her daughter wasn't where she was supposed to be.

"Mallory, did you take my pen?"

Mrs. Sutton's voice carried through the house and Mallory sighed before raising her voice in response. "No. Why would I take your pen, Mom?"

"To write with."

Mallory chuckled and dropped her forehead against Irish's chest. "Save me."

He rubbed her back and planted a kiss on the top of her head. "A few more hours and you can sneak out of here."

Her body relaxed so much, he thought if he stepped back, she might fall down. "I'll try to stay awake."

"You're really setting the bar high for me here, Mallory. I don't know if I can take that kind of pressure."

She laughed and stood straight as her mother called her name again. "You should go. Save yourself."

"I'm afraid I'm going to spend the night pacing the floor in my camper because you sat down for two seconds and fell asleep."

"No chance, cowboy." She took a step away because her mother's voice was getting closer, but the look she gave him was as potent as a touch. "You and me? That's happening."

Chapter Ten

There was a question from Debbie M. in our comments, asking how to deal with a mama bear and her cub using her kiddie pool to cool off, so we asked the Stonefield Police Department for a response. It was (and we quote): "Don't offer them snacks. They'll never leave." (But have no fear, they've reached out to NH Fish & Game for help.) Making sure all food and garbage is secured is always good advice, though!

—*Stonefield Gazette* Facebook Page

Mallory would have felt like a teenager again, sneaking out to meet a boy, except she'd never snuck out when she was younger. Here she was for the first time, a grown woman—a mother of two, for goodness' sake—tiptoeing down the stairs while avoiding all the creaky spots and hoping nobody left anything out that might trip her in the dark.

A rectangle of dim light led her across the drive to the open camper door, and when Irish saw her through the screen door, he stood. His shirt was untucked and unbuttoned, giving her a tantalizing glimpse of his broad chest and taut stomach. His feet were bare, and she could see his hat sitting on the island.

She opened the door and he held out his hand so she could hold on to him as she climbed the steps. He had to step aside so she could get by him, and then he reached out to pull the solid door closed. There was no book in his hand. No television on. It looked to her as though he'd been doing nothing but waiting for her.

She kicked her sandals off so they landed on the small mat with his boots. He locked the door.

Mallory hadn't expected to be nervous, but she could feel the telltale blush across her chest when his eyes met hers. "Hi."

His eyes crinkled and he brushed her hair back from her face. "Howdy, ma'am."

The extra drawl he put into it, as though he was from Texas and not Montana, made her laugh and she knew he'd done it deliberately to pop the bubble of awkwardness. And it worked. Nervousness gave way to desire as he hooked his hand around her waist and pulled her close. She slid her fingers under his open shirt so there was no barrier between her hands and his chest as he lowered his head to kiss her.

Finally, she thought. Finally she could lose herself in this man's kisses—in his touch—and not worry about who was around the corner or who might see them or hear them. They were alone and she was free to focus all of her attention on Irish.

He pulled his head back, and she had to stifle an annoyed whimper. "It feels rude to not offer you a drink or something before I pounce on you like this."

"All I want is you," she assured him, pushing his shirt off of his shoulders so it could fall to the ground. Now the only thing between their chests was *her* shirt, and she hoped to be losing that soon.

He kissed her again, this time claiming her mouth so thoroughly, he took her breath away. She held on to him, her hands sliding up his naked back as his explored the curves of her hips and ass. When his hands moved under the hem of the oversize T-shirt she slept in and his hands touched the bare flesh of her back, she sucked in a breath.

But he released her mouth, resting his forehead against hers. "Promise me you'll tell me if my hands are too harsh for you. I've been putting hand cream on them, but they're still really rough and your skin is very soft."

"That was a 'finally, his hands on my body' sound, not an *ow* sound. Your hands are fine."

"Maybe for little bit, but if I keep touching a spot or something—"

"I promise I'll tell you." A couple of times recently, she'd thought she smelled fruit when she was near Irish, and now she realized he'd been using the apricot hand lotion in the downstairs bathroom of the house.

Just so his hands wouldn't be too rough for her.

For a man who looked hard and unemotional on the outside, he sure was a softie on the inside. And a lot of people liked him, but she got a little thrill out of being the only person who knew just how truly sweet he was.

And she put that thrilled feeling into kissing him because distracting him from worrying about his hands being rough was the best way to ensure he wasn't shy about running those hands all over her body. She caught his bottom lip between her teeth, biting just hard enough to elicit a low groan from him, and then she slid her tongue over his.

Part of her wanted to move on toward the bedroom, or at least the love seat, but that would mean stopping the kissing and letting go of him. Standing wasn't so bad, really.

"I guess we could stop standing here in front of the door," he lifted his mouth from her neck to say, as though he'd read her mind. "Not doing a great job of inviting you in."

"I think you did a pretty good job of welcoming me in, actually."

His eyes crinkled at the corners. "At least we can skip the awkward part where you have to ask me if I have protection."

"One of the benefits of living in a small town."

Irish stepped back and took her hand, but he only took one step toward his bedroom before he stopped, uncertainty making his brow furrow. She could only too well imagine him trying to decide if he was supposed to sit and talk with her first, maybe offer her a snack. He'd hung back before, waiting for her to make the first move, and if that's what was happening, she had no problem doing so again.

Mallory pulled her fingers from Irish's grasp so she had both hands free to pull the T-shirt off and toss it away. She gave him a moment to register that she wasn't wearing a bra—and to savor the way his breath caught when he saw her naked breasts—and then she turned and walked away.

She was pretty sure he'd follow.

When she reached the top of two steps leading to his bedroom, she paused. The sleep pants she wore were on the looser side, so all she had to do was tug the bow out of the drawstring and they fell to her feet. Stepping out of the pooled fabric, she tried to fake a confidence she didn't totally feel.

Maybe it would have been easier if she was wearing a supersexy lingerie set made of lace and strategically hidden supports. But she didn't own any and she didn't want to spend the money to order some. Plus, Irish wouldn't care—he'd even wanted her when she was a hot mess in old yoga pants.

When she reached the end of the bed, she took a deep breath and turned, expecting him to be right behind her. He was still standing at the bottom of the steps. Her instinct was to cover herself with her hands—she'd had two kids and really liked carbs—but the look in his eyes stopped her. He definitely didn't care that she didn't have pretty lace holding everything in place.

"Are you going to join me?"

His response was a sound that left no doubt he liked what he saw, and then he closed the distance between them. Then he lifted her and set her in the center of the bed before climbing in and lowering himself over her.

"You planning to take off those jeans, cowboy?"

"Yes, ma'am," he said. "But not just yet."

"I know you like to take your time about things, but—" She gasped when his mouth closed over her nipple and sucked hard. "Oh."

That was the last coherent sound to come out of her mouth for a while as Irish showed her just how intoxicating slow and deliberate could be. His mouth—framed by the soft mustache and beard—

and his calloused hands touched her everywhere. Her neck. Her breasts. Her stomach. The soft skin of her inner thighs and the sensitive flesh between them. It wasn't until after he brought her to orgasm, his tongue doing masterful things with her clit, that he finally stood and pushed his jeans down.

He was as magnificent as she'd imagined him. Every muscle in his body had been hardened by a lifetime of hard work. Except the one that was hardened by wanting her. That was magnificent, too, she thought as she grinned in anticipation while he rolled a condom on.

"You took your time touching me," she said. "But you're not going let me return the favor?"

"Sweetheart, I've been wanting you for a while now. You can do whatever makes you happy, but if it involves your mouth on me, it's going to end well for me, but you might be disappointed."

It was on the tip of her tongue to point out she was already well on her way to a satisfied night's sleep, but she didn't because she wanted to feel him inside of her.

After he settled between her thighs, he stilled for a moment, staring into her eyes. There was heat, but there was also a different kind of warmth in the blue depths, and she couldn't help stroking his cheek. Then he reached down and guided himself into her, and she slid that hand around to the back of his neck.

As he slowly pushed into her, going a little deeper with each thrust, she ran her fingers up into his hair.

"Is this okay?" he asked in a hoarse voice as he paused, his erection filling her completely.

"Okay is an understatement."

His mouth quirked up at the corners and he started to move, slowly at first. She closed her eyes, letting the sensations envelop her. He kissed her neck, then her jaw and finally claimed her mouth while he rolled one taut nipple between his thumb and finger.

She heard his breathing and felt the trembling of his muscles under her fingers, and knew he was exerting a lot of self-control. He thrust harder and faster, and when she wrapped her legs around him, he hooked his arm under one of her knees and lifted. Opened farther to him, she gasped as he went deeper.

When he moaned, she reached between their bodies and stroked her clit until she came, her back arching off the bed. Almost immediately, his muscles tightened and he groaned as his orgasm shook his body. He thrust in uneven strokes until it passed and then he slowly lowered himself onto her.

Mallory wrapped her arms and legs around him, holding him close while they caught their breath. He kissed her temple twice before burying his face in her neck. She knew he'd have to get up in a moment and discard the condom, but she wasn't ready to let him go quite yet.

"I don't think you were too loud at all," he said, making her laugh.

"Good. It would be really awkward if somebody heard us out here."

He lifted his head to kiss her jaw. "Don't worry. I'd just tell them I was watching porn on my laptop."

She laughed again, and then turned her head so she could brush her lips against his. "You're so sweet."

Irish had added a couple extra pillows to the bed earlier in the evening. At the time, he'd been afraid of Mallory hitting her head on the nightstand cabinet because the room was definitely a close-quarters situation. But now they were cuddling against the nest of pillows, and he figured it had been one of the best ideas he'd ever had.

"I needed that," she said, stretching her body without leaving the curve of his arm. "I'm really glad you decided to park your camper here."

"Me too." He trailed his fingertips over her arm. "And I'm glad the men in this town don't seem to share half a brain between them."

Mallory laughed, shaking her head. "And you know that from all ten minutes of nonbartending interaction you've had with other people in Stonefield? Other than Case or Lane, of course, because I don't think you're talking about them."

"I don't mean them, and I don't need to interact

with anybody. If any of the men in this town were smart, you wouldn't be single."

As sweet as the sentiment was, she rolled her eyes. "As if it's their decision."

He gave a single nod of his head. "Point taken."

"I've dated since the divorce, obviously. I mean, it's been years. In the beginning, I had my hands full putting my life back together again, but then I started going out once in a while. I did have one relationship that I thought was serious—the single dad I told you about. We had a lot in common and the kids got along pretty well."

"What changed? Was it this?" He pointed in the direction of the taproom, even though they couldn't see it with the curtains closed.

"No, it ended a couple of years before all this even started. At some point I realized that it wasn't about real emotional connection for him. He thought what we had in common was that I needed a father for my kids as much as he needed a mother for the times he had *his* kids. Having me in his life made it easier for him as a single parent and that was enough for him. It wasn't enough for me."

"And you haven't dated since then?"

"Nope. That relationship ending was very discouraging, and it was hard on Jack and Eli. Getting us back on track kept me busy. Then my dad and Lane started working on this place and everything changed—especially after my dad died. I haven't had the energy or the time to even think about dating."

He made a sound that was almost a chuckle. "I guess it was pretty smart of me to camp right in your backyard, then."

"You did make it easy," she said, and he heard the teasing in her voice. But then her expression grew serious, and almost sad, which he didn't like seeing. "You never smile, even when I think I'm being funny."

He'd heard that before, often before whatever woman he was in a temporary relationship with decided it was over. "It doesn't mean I'm not happy or not enjoying myself."

"I just don't think I've ever met somebody who doesn't smile and laugh before."

He didn't want to talk about his childhood, if it could even be called that. That ugliness should have no part of this beautiful day with this beautiful woman, and he wasn't the kind of guy who liked to spend a lot of time looking in his rearview mirror. The idea that Mallory might think he wasn't enjoying her company didn't sit right with him, though.

"My family wasn't like yours is," he said quietly. "In my house, your emotions got used against you. We worked from before the sun came up until after the sun went down, just trying to keep a useless piece of land and the bare minimum of food on the table. There was no time for playing and laughing, and if my mother or I looked happy, my father felt like it was his duty to remind us we had nothing to be happy about. And if we didn't look happy, we needed an attitude adjustment. After my mom died, he got worse and there were times not giving away what I was thinking really felt like life or death. At the very least, it kept me from getting beat."

"I'm sorry." Mallory wrapped both of her hands around his, and the strength he felt there was almost worth picking at the old wounds. "You don't have to talk about it."

"I don't really have anything else to say about it. They've both been gone a long time." He stared down at their intertwined hands for a few seconds before looking back at her. "I feel everything. Your family makes me feel welcome and I love hearing you laugh and it makes me happy being around you. I feel it, even though you can't see it in me because old habits are hard to break."

"Oh, I can see it," she said, smiling. "It's subtle and can be hard to see because of the beard situation, but the corners of your mouth turn up just a little so it's not a smile, but I can see it. And you get a little sparkle in your eyes, too."

"I do, huh?" A wave of emotion made his body tighten, and for a few seconds he thought he might end up with tears in his eyes.

Then she laughed again and he really wished he

could make himself just let go and laugh with her. "Yes, you do. I see you, Irish."

Shit. There was that emotion again. He did the only thing he could do to hold back the effect her words were having on him—he kissed her. Slowly. Thoroughly. He kissed her until there was no past and no future, but just this one perfect moment he wanted to live in forever.

The kiss led to them making love again, and then he wanted nothing more than to curl his body around hers and fall asleep to the soft sound of her breathing. But she had to go, and they both knew it. Even if they woke up early and she was able to sneak back in to the house without anybody seeing her, he knew it was bothering her that the boys didn't know where she was. Evie knew, but Jack or Eli looking for Mallory in the middle of the night would probably end with everybody in the house looking for her. It wouldn't be the end of the world, but he knew she didn't want them all in her business.

"I need to go before I fall asleep," she said as she pulled her shirt over her head and slid out of his bed. "I need to be awake enough to remember where all the creaky floorboards are."

"Lane's going to have me come up with a limited-edition brew, which will keep me here about a month, so maybe you'll get some practice." He said the words casually, but his insides knotted up as he waited to see her reaction to the hint they could do this again. And again.

She paused in the act of making sure she was decent to smile at him. “About a month seems like the perfect length for a fun fling.”

“Seems like it.”

“Okay, I really have to go,” she said. He threw back the blanket, intending to get up, but she shook her head. “There’s no sense in you getting up.”

He got up anyway, pulling on the jeans that had ended up on the floor. “I know I can’t walk you to your door, but I’m going to kiss you goodbye.”

“Just a kiss,” she said, pointing her finger at him. “I can’t end up back in that bed, no matter how much I want to.”

It wasn’t easy, but he gave her one scorching good-night kiss, and then let her walk out the door. She gave him a little wave before walking across the drive, and he was back in his bed and peeking out the window at the head of it in time to see her duck into the house. She caught the screen door, making sure it didn’t slam and then, after a final look in his direction, she closed the big door.

The pillow her head had rested on still held the faint scent of her shampoo, and he allowed himself a very small smile as he fell asleep with the pillow held against his cheek.

Chapter Eleven

At the selectmen's meeting, a motion to rename High Street due to recurring thefts of the street sign was unanimously passed. Not only does replacing the sign cost the taxpayers money, but it's important for street signs to be in place so the residents can be found by 911 first responders and Amazon Prime delivery drivers. Suggestions for a new name will be accepted at town hall and via an upcoming online form, but be aware all suggestions will be run through a Google search to ensure no inappropriate slang is missed by selectmen.

—*Stonefield Gazette* Facebook Page

For two weeks, Irish went along with Mallory's road map for their relationship. They went about their daily lives, sneaking time alone together when they could. They spent a *lot* of time together, actually. But there were usually other people around, which meant hands off.

He didn't like keeping his hands off Mallory.

And he wanted to take her away from everything, even if just for a day. Between the thrift shop and the taproom and her family, she never got a break. No matter how much she was juggling, there was always something else she thought she could be doing, and he wanted her to relax. He wanted to pamper her—maybe spoil her a little bit—but he couldn't figure out a way to do it.

The answer finally came during a cookout in the backyard. It still felt weird to have barbecues on a Monday night, but it was the one day of the week the Sutton women didn't have to work. They'd just finished eating when Irish's phone buzzed in his pocket. He walked toward the house to take the call, and was standing by the back door to the kitchen when Mallory walked by with the tray of condiments to put away.

When she came back out, he was slipping the phone in his pocket and she smiled, but didn't ask him who he was talking to. He was going to tell her anyway, since he thought it was good news. After glancing around to make sure they were still alone, he gestured for her to come closer.

"That was the oceanfront campground in Maine

I've been on a waiting list for since two days before I left Montana," he said. "They had a cancellation for this coming weekend and I'm up."

"Oh, that's right. You wanted to see the ocean and you haven't yet."

"I'm going to hook up the camper and go while I have the chance."

She smiled. "That sounds fun. Especially in a camper. I've always wanted to take the boys to the ocean for more than a day trip, but it's so expensive to stay on the coast."

It was the wistful tone that made up his mind for him. "Go with me."

Her eyes widened. "What?"

"Go to the ocean with me. You and the boys."

"The water is still *really* cold this early in the year."

"We're tough guys. We can swim—or at least wade in the water—for a few minutes. And I'm not all that big on swimming, anyway. We can explore the area. Find shells. Have a campfire." He did miss the crackle of an open fire. "I think the boys would have a great time."

"They would." But she didn't sound convinced it was a good idea. "I don't know. I mean, that doesn't sound like a very friends-with-benefits thing to do, if you know what I mean."

He tilted his head. "Who says the benefit always

has to be sex? Maybe the benefit can be a weekend at the ocean."

"I..." She wanted to. He could see it on her face. "But remember what I said about the boys getting attached to you?"

"Yeah. I also remember you telling me that Case and Lane have taken them to do fun stuff, and I'm pretty sure you've gone along a time or two. This doesn't have to be any different than that."

She gave him a skeptical look. "Where would everybody sleep?"

"There are two options." He wanted to respect the fact she might not be ready to sleep in his bed with her sons around, even if he promised they'd only sleep. "One option is you sleeping in my bed while I keep my hands to myself and the boys sleep on the love seat, which pulls out."

"I one hundred percent believe you have the willpower to share a bed with me and keep your hands to yourself. But I don't have your superhuman level of self-discipline, so what's option two?"

Even if it made planning their trip more difficult, he liked the fact she didn't think she could keep her hands off of him. "You three take the camper at night and I'll throw up a tent to sleep in."

She frowned. "You can't sleep in a tent. It's chilly at night on the coast, even in the summer, because of the ocean breeze."

"I've spent more nights than you can imagine

sleeping on the ground, with or without a tent. I still have my bedroll in the closet of my camper."

"I don't know. There are always a million things to do and my family—"

"Do you *want* to go to the ocean with me? That's the question."

"Yes." She looked surprised to have answered the question so quickly, but then he could see all the *but*s piling up. "I want to. I mean, *of course* I'd love to take the boys camping with you, especially to the ocean, but—"

"Then we'll go."

"I can't just go. There's the brewery and the thrift shop and somebody always needs me for something."

He wasn't going to get anywhere like this. She would keep circling around all the things that needed doing and talk herself out of it, but he'd heard what he needed to hear. Mallory wanted to go, so she was going. It was that simple.

Turning, he walked back to the gazebo, where the rest of the family—minus Jack and Eli, who'd run off to play with Boomer—was still gathered around the table. "Mallory wants to take the boys camping and I still want to see the ocean, so I'd like to take them with me this coming weekend. She wouldn't be available from after the boys get home from school on Friday until late afternoon on Sunday, if you can make that work."

He waited, giving anybody a chance to object

even though it wouldn't do them any good, but after a long moment of silence and a few glances at each other across the table, it was Gwen who finally broke the silence. "Case and I have nothing going on this weekend, so we can cover for her."

"The boys will love that," Ellen said, giving him a warm smile. "Do you know where you're going yet?"

"Yes, ma'am." Everybody waited, and he knew he couldn't run off with her daughter and grandsons without letting her know where they were going. "I have a reservation on the coast of Maine."

They all looked pleased, including Mallory, who'd followed him to the gazebo. He knew there was a good chance her family was going to read more into the trip than Mallory might want them to, but maybe if the boys reported back that Irish had slept in a tent, it might help lay that to rest.

But the bottom line was that he didn't really care what her family thought. If he had to move on soon to keep what he and Mallory had from getting too painfully messy, he wanted her to have this trip with her boys first.

And he wanted memories that he could hold close to his heart when he was alone again.

Mallory wasn't surprised when both boys had nodded off less than an hour into the two-hour drive to the oceanfront campground where Irish had told her they were staying. They were so excited about this adventure, she'd had a hard time getting them to bed last night, and Evie, who shared a bathroom with them, said neither of them had gone right to sleep. Then they'd gotten up at dawn and judging by the way they'd been as wound up when they got home as when they left for school, she should probably send their teacher a gift card to the coffee shop. They hadn't calmed down until they got bored with the passing scenery and finally nodded off.

She didn't blame them. She'd had a hard time sleeping herself, since she'd spent half the night asking herself if she was sure this camping trip—the *family* trip to the beach vibe—was a good idea.

It probably wasn't.

She didn't think Jack and Eli thought too much about it. They had a big family—actual relatives and otherwise—so there was always somebody doing something with them. Case and Lane took them along for different activities and this time it just happened to be Irish. They'd probably just lumped him in with everybody else, if they even thought about it at all, just like he'd said they would.

But Mallory knew it was different.

If this was a real relationship and not a fling with a cowboy who was just passing through town—even though he was passing through a lot slower than they'd both anticipated—this trip would be a major milestone.

Instead, they were at around the halfway point—

or maybe a little past it—of the month or so Irish had told her he'd be staying around while he worked on a special beer for the brewery. The clock was ticking away, and most of the time it felt like it was going too fast. But sometimes, when she realized how much she wished their relationship was real, it felt like it was passing too quickly for her own good.

Putting that thought out of her mind, she leaned her head against the seat and sighed with contentment. She hadn't had a real vacation since before the boys were born, and she was going to soak in every second of relaxation she could.

Mallory had taken the day off from the thrift store so she and Irish could grab some groceries and pack the camper—taking a quick break to make love while nobody else was around—so their duffel bags were already inside. There was a very short window of time between the boys getting home from school and the taproom opening, and he'd made it very clear he wanted to be out of there during that time. He was afraid once they opened the doors, Mallory would get sucked into working.

But once she'd told Jack and Eli they were coming here, she wouldn't have changed her mind.

"How long, do you think, between me turning the truck off and them asking to go in the water?" he asked after merging into highway traffic.

She smiled. "It's funny that you think they'll wait until you turn the truck off."

"Can't blame them. I'm pretty excited about being in the ocean myself."

"You do know you're going to look out of place in jeans and cowboy boots on the beach, right?"

He gave her an affronted look. "I have swim trunks."

For some reason, that really surprised her. "Did you already have a pair, or did you buy them for this weekend?"

He glanced over at her again, shook his head, and then turned his attention back to the road. "I already had them. People swim in Montana, you know."

She knew him too well to fall for that. "But have *you* worn them to swim? Or did you buy them just before you left, when you put your name on the waiting list for an oceanfront campground?"

He drummed his fingers on the steering wheel, deliberately not looking at her. And when he stroked his hand over his mustache and beard, she wondered if he was actually trying to hold back a smile. And even though she understood why he'd do that, there was a part of her that wished he trusted her with that part of himself—that he could share his emotions with her.

And his name, for that matter. The closer they got, the more she wanted to make sure he just didn't like the other half of his given name and wasn't hiding anything in his past. That information was something she needed him to trust her with.

"When I wanted to swim, I just stripped down and jumped in," he finally admitted, and the image of that had her wishing there was a little more air conditioning pumping out of the truck's vents.

"As fun as that would be to watch," she said, "especially considering how cold the water will be, that would probably cut our vacation short."

"Frown on naked cowboys in the ocean, do they?"

"It's the naked cowboys on the beach that are the problem."

He shook his head. "Nothing better than diving naked into a cold lake after a long, hot day."

Mallory shivered, being more of a *dip the toe and then ease in slowly* kind of swimmer. "I'll have to take your word for it."

The boys woke up when they stopped for diesel, and they saw the fast food sign. Mallory was about to remind them they had coolers full of food when Irish beckoned for her to get out of the truck. After telling the boys to sit tight, she walked around to the fuel pump.

He turned his back to the window the boys were watching them through and kept his voice low. "Did you want to grab a bite while we're here? I didn't want to ask you in front of them because then they'd never let you say no."

She appreciated that he hadn't put her in that position. "We brought more than enough food."

"But do you want to finish setting up and then

have to make supper and then clean up? Or do you want to get there and have nothing to do but sit and look at the ocean?"

"I try to limit the fast food."

"But it's vacation. It'll be a treat for the boys and less work for you when we get there."

She put her hands on her hips. "You're going to spoil them."

"They deserve it. So do you."

That got her. The boys had been so good since their grandfather died and all the grown-ups in their lives had thrown all their energy into opening the brewery and taproom. She surrendered and once the truck was full, Irish parked it and they walked to get something to eat. There was a small connector road they had to cross, and Mallory saw Eli slip his hand into Irish's before they stepped off the sidewalk.

Luckily, she managed to blink away the moisture in her eyes before he held the door open for her. The boys already liked him so much, and she was so torn between letting Jack and Eli have that bond with him and needing to pull them back so they wouldn't be as hurt when Irish left. But she already liked him so much, too, and she couldn't make herself hold him at a distance—for her *or* the boys.

Hopped up on junk food and soda, Jack and Eli had no trouble staying awake for the rest of the ride. As anxious as the boys were to get their weekend started, Irish made them sit in the truck until they were fully parked. Mallory was ready to get out and help direct him, but it didn't seem like he needed the help. If he'd backed the camper along the carriage house as easily as he backed into their campsite, it was no wonder nobody in the house had woken up.

When they finally spilled out of the truck, she expected the boys to start running around, checking everything out and seeing if there were other kids to play with, but they stood one on either side of her. They stared at the water and then Eli looked up at her.

"This is where we're staying? For the whole weekend?" When she nodded, he grinned. "This is so cool. The ocean is right there!"

"It's very cool," she said. "And if either of you so much as put a foot in that water without me or Irish, you'll spend the entire weekend sitting in the camper. That's the number-one rule. You do *not* go in the water without a grown-up."

While Irish set up the camper, she went over a few more rules with the boys. They had gone tent camping a few times, but this was their first time in a proper campground so they needed to know the basics about respecting others' campsites and noise levels and everything else she could think of.

"Can we go swimming now?" Jack asked when she was done talking.

"That water is so cold," she said. "The news even talked about how cold the water still is."

"Just for a few minutes." Eli gave her puppy-dog eyes. "Please, Mom? You don't have to go in. You can just watch us."

"Nope. It's not a pool, so there are currents and riptides. You're not going in alone."

"I'll go in with them."

She turned to see Irish had finished with the camper and had joined them at the line of spaced-out boulders that marked the line between the campground and the beach. "You do know that water's cold, right?"

"You've said that at least twenty-six times today, but we didn't come here to sit and read, Mallory."

"I did."

The boys were silent, knowing Irish would make a stronger case with their mother, but they had their hands clasped in front of their chests and were bouncing up and down on the balls of their feet. She was used to resisting them, but when Irish mimicked them—clasping his hands and bouncing twice while giving her a pleading look—she lost the battle.

"Fine," she said, unable to hold back her laughter. "Go. Freeze. Get everything wet and sandy for the whole forty-five seconds you'll actually be in the water."

They all went in to change, and it was no surprise the boys burst out of the camper first. They were in bright swim trunks with towels draped around their necks and water shoes on their feet. And the grins.

They looked like they were about to explode with excitement, and she chuckled when she thought about how they were going to shriek when they actually hit the water.

"Hurry up, Irish," Jack yelled, even though it had only been about twenty seconds since they exited the camper.

"Sunscreen," she said.

"Mom, it's not even hot."

"Water reflects the sun, so even though it's not high in the sky and you have a little color already, you can burn. Sunscreen or you sit in the shade with me."

With a lot of grumbling and hissing at the cold lotion, even though she tried to warm it in her hands first, they succumbed to being coated in lotion. And she was just finishing up when the camper door opened again and Irish stepped out.

She'd seen his body before, of course, but indoors and in dim lighting. It was different when he stepped out of the camper and the sun reflected off his very white legs. She had to cover her mouth to keep from laughing at loud, but of course the gesture gave her away. She wasn't sure if his lower body had ever seen the sun.

"What so funny?" He was scowling, but the mustache and beard didn't hide the way his lips tilted up at the corners. Not a lot, but she could see the almost smile.

"You are going to need a *lot* of sunscreen."

"You can apply as much as you want, as often as you want," he said, and she realized she was still holding the bottle she'd used on the boys.

"I think you can do your own legs."

"What about my back?" He was walking slowly toward her and the look in his eyes made her glad there was a slight breeze to cool the back of her neck.

"You're a little tan there," she told him. "You must work without a shirt sometimes, so I don't think you'll burn. And the sun's on its way down."

"You told Jack and Eli the water reflects the sun and they could burn easier than usual, even if you're already tanned and the sun's going down. I was listening. Do you want me to burn, Mallory?"

He gave her a look that should have melted her clothes right off her body, and she knew he was doing it on purpose. "Fine. I'll do your back. Turn around."

Because he'd given her that look, she didn't bother rubbing the lotion in her palms first. She slapped a big dollop on his back and laughed when he hissed and tried to arch away from her.

"You did that on purpose."

She smiled and rubbed the lotion over his back. She loved the muscles there, and the way they tensed under her touch.

"Irish, come *on*," the boys wailed in unison.

"You're done," she told him. "I'm going to go

wash this sunscreen off my hands so I can sit and read in peace."

As soon as she stepped into the camper, she saw it.

His wallet was on the counter, along with a pocketknife and keys, so he'd probably tossed everything there before changing into his swim trunks. He seemed like the kind of guy to tuck them away in a drawer, but he might have been hurrying for the sake of her impatient sons.

She stared at the battered brown leather billfold, her fingertips itching to touch it—to flip it open and see what was inside. His driver's license would be in there and, regardless of what he preferred being called, his ID would have his full legal name on it.

Of course she wanted to know his name. But she didn't want to just *know* it. She wanted him to tell her himself—to trust her enough to share that information with her. There was a story there, but it was his to tell. And the only way she wanted to hear the story was from his lips.

After washing her hands, she grabbed the paperback she'd taken from the thrift shop in anticipation of the weekend and went back outside just in time to hear Eli shriek when Jack splashed him. She'd told them about screaming, but she also knew the water was frigid, so she let it slide. The rule was that they could only go up to their armpits, but she'd be surprised if they got their knees wet tonight.

While he'd been setting up, Irish had pulled four

folding camp chairs out of one of the camper's many storage compartments, so she popped one open and settled in with her book. She didn't open it, though.

It was too much fun watching Irish wading in the ocean with her boys.

Irish had always loved the sound of an open fire. The crackling and popping of the wood. A hissing sound when the flames found a pocket of moisture. They were sounds he'd always found particularly soothing, and listening to a fire was one of his favorite ways to fall asleep.

He'd never sat next to a campfire with two young boys who weren't great at sitting still, though. His nerves were shot, and he was pretty sure if he took off his hat and looked in a mirror, he'd find some gray streaks in his hair.

And Mallory had abandoned him, retreating into the camper to set up the love seat so the boys could go to bed. Eventually. If they ever stopped moving.

"Can we put more wood on the fire?" Eli asked, because the fire was definitely his favorite part. He kept poking it with the long stick they'd found, and he'd only accidentally set the tip on fire twice.

"No, dummy," Jack said. "If the fire's too high we can't toast marshmallows because they just burn up."

"Don't call your brother names," Irish said in a low voice.

"Sorry," Jack said, looking contrite.

"But Jack's right," Irish continued. "Your mom bought marshmallows, so you don't want the fire too high."

"She got chocolate, too," Eli told him. "And graham crackers, so we can make s'mores."

"You like s'mores, right?" Jack asked.

"Never had one."

The ensuing silence went on longer than was normal for the boys, and then Jack leaned forward in his chair, squinting at Irish. He wasn't sure if the kid thought he might be an alien of some sort or if he was trying to detect a lie on Irish's face. "You've never had s'mores?"

"Nope."

They both jumped up faster than Irish would have thought possible from a folding camp chair—taking about five years off his life as he prayed they wouldn't trip and fall in the firepit—and ran for the camper, with Eli yelling, *"Moooooom!"*

Irish shook his head, not sure how a kid could turn three simple letters into one of the longest words he'd ever heard, but it was one of Eli's stronger skills.

"Irish has never had a s'more," Jack was yelling as the two boys jostled at the camper stairs, each trying to be the one who broke the headline news.

"Boys, there are other campers and they don't want to hear you yelling." Mallory appeared on the other side of the screen, using that tone mothers seemed to have that wasn't loud as decibels went, but stopped the kids in their tracks.

"But Irish has never had a s'more," Eli said in the loudest whisper Irish had ever heard. "We have to make him one *right now.*"

"You don't have to whisper," Mallory said. "Just don't yell. And before you get too excited, did you ask Irish if he even *wants* to try a s'more?"

"Irish, do you want a s'more?" Eli asked him, forgetting to whisper.

"You have to," Jack said. "They're the best thing in the whole world."

Sweets weren't really Irish's thing—give him something spicy any day—and he knew just enough about s'mores to know he was going to end up with melted marshmallow in his beard, but he wasn't about to disappoint the two young boys giving him intensely hopeful looks, as though they truly believed they were about to change his life for the better. "I could try one."

Eli pressed his face to the screen. "He wants a s'more, Mom."

"I heard him. I'm almost done here and then I'll bring the stuff out."

Irish used Eli's stick to knock the fire down a little more, spreading the hot bed of coals around. He'd probably throw a couple more logs in, but he'd wait until after the s'mores were done because he could too easily imagine a flaming, molten marshmallow being flung from the end of a stick.

He never would have guessed how much effort went into just *getting ready* to make s'mores. He'd been wondering how they were going to find marshmallow sticks since there wasn't a tree in sight, but Mallory had a package of bamboo sticks in her bag. Then she made an assembly line on the picnic table—marshmallows, a chocolate bar broken into pieces, an open package of graham crackers and a package of baby wipes.

Once she had it all laid out, she put her hands on her hips and sighed. "I think we should apologize to Irish in advance."

"Sorry, Irish," both boys said at the same time, and she laughed since she obviously hadn't meant it literally.

Hovering over them, Mallory oversaw the toasting of the marshmallows, reminding them to turn the sticks and not to get too close to the flickering embers. When they were done, she was ready. After setting a piece of chocolate on top of a graham cracker, she held it out to Eli. He set his marshmallow on top of the chocolate, and once she put another graham cracker on top of that, she nodded and he pulled the stick out. She repeated the process for Jack.

It was Eli who brought Irish his first s'more. He took it carefully, not wanting to crush it into a gooey mess, but with his first bite he realized that was inevitable. He expected Eli to rush back to Mallory to make one for himself, but he stared at Irish, waiting for the verdict. Jack's was cooling in his hand while he waited, too.

Once he'd swallowed the sweet, sticky mess, he nodded. "This is really something."

Both boys beamed at him, and Jack said, "I can make you another one after mine."

"I'm going to take my time eating this one, to make it last. You go ahead."

He saw Mallory's knowing grin and shook his head. But he took another bite because he was going to eat the entire thing if it killed him. And it might. A string of marshmallow fell onto his beard, and he shuddered to think what he must look like.

But he couldn't look any worse than Eli and Jack, who seemed to get as much melted marshmallow on their faces and hands as they did in their mouths.

"You want a bite of mine since you're busy with them?" he asked Mallory, hoping for a reprieve.

"Mom doesn't like s'mores because they're messy," Jack said. "She just sneaks pieces of the chocolate while we're toasting our marshmallows."

A guilty blush gave her away, and he arched an eyebrow at her. "I didn't know that was an option."

He was teasing her, of course. He wouldn't disappoint Jack and Eli by not eating the s'more they'd been so excited about, but he was relieved when—after they'd each had two—Mallory said it was enough. She handed out baby wipes so they could clean themselves up enough to get inside to wash thoroughly with hot water, and she was grinning when she handed him several.

"You might have to get a bowl of hot water and just prop your chin in it for a while."

"I think us menfolk should head to the bathhouse because we're going to need more hot water than that camper can make. Although smelling like a baby's butt is a new experience for me."

The boys laughed and started making jokes about baby butts, so he herded them toward the bathhouse before he got blamed for that. By the time they'd scrubbed all the marshmallow and chocolate off themselves, she had everything put away and had put another log on the fire.

"You can watch this one burn," she told the boys, "And then it's time for bed."

Eli barely made it, despite the sugar he'd consumed, and Jack didn't even argue when she told them to say good-night to Irish. While he liked seeing them enjoy themselves, he was exhausted, and he threw another log on because all he wanted to do now was sit and stare at the fire.

It took her about twenty minutes to get them settled onto the pulled-out love seat, and when she had climbed down the steps and closed the door behind her, she gave a sigh that seemed to come from the depths of her soul.

"They're both sound asleep already," she said in a low voice when she reached the fire. "They really needed this."

She moved her chair three times—sitting down and then getting up again—and he was about to ask her what the problem was when she finally settled and reached out to take his hand. He got it then. She'd made it so they could sit together in front of the fire without their joined hands being visible to a child who might have trouble sleeping and look out the camper window.

Maybe liking him being a secret she was so determined to keep should have bothered him more, but he appreciated how hard she worked to find these small ways to connect with him. And sitting in front of the crackling flames holding Mallory's hand was close to the most perfect night he'd ever had.

"This is amazing," she said in a low voice after a few minutes. "I feel so bad about you sleeping in a tent, though."

"I told you, I'm used to sleeping in tents." He'd already set it up and pulled his bedroll out of the storage compartment. He hadn't been sure he'd ever use it again, but he hadn't been able to part with it, which he was thankful for now. "And it's worth it to see you like this, with the fire shining on your hair."

Her head was leaned against the back of the camp chair, but she swiveled it to give him a smile that warmed him even more than the fire could. "I can't remember the last time I felt this relaxed. And that's not an exaggeration. I literally don't remember feeling so…peaceful. Not for a very long time."

"That's why we're here."

"Was it everything you thought it would be? The ocean, I mean?"

"Seeing it was worth the drive," he said, looking out over the expanse of dark water. "Pretty damn cold, though."

"You guys were in longer than I thought you would be. I gave you forty-five seconds."

"If it was just me, you would have won that bet. Those boys, though. Eli was standing there with his whole body shivering, his teeth chattering and his lips turning blue, trying to convince me he wasn't cold."

She laughed softly and he squeezed her hand. He considered putting another log on the fire, but it wasn't long before Mallory was so relaxed, she was yawning. And when she pulled her sweater closer around her body, he knew the chilly, damp air was getting to her.

"Go in and go to bed," he said softly. "It was a long day and I think we'll both need our rest to keep up with them tomorrow."

"I really want to stay here with you, like this," she said, and his heart did a funny thump in his chest. "But you're right. And I'm going to fall asleep if I keep sitting here, and I think you trying to fit through that camper door carrying me would wake everybody up."

He pushed himself out of the chair and then helped her get to her feet. She looked into his eyes for a long moment while he savored the feel of her hand in his and the moonlight reflecting in her eyes, and then she smiled.

"Good night, Irish."

"Good night, Mallory." When her hand slid free of his, he closed his fingers into a fist as if he could hold on to the sensation longer, and he watched her until she was inside.

After putting the fire out and setting the folded-up chairs under the awning in case it rained, he made a quick run to the bathhouse and then climbed into his tent. Making himself comfortable in the old, familiar bedroll, he tucked his hands under his head and stared up at the canvas.

Today had been a very good day. One of the best he'd ever had and now that it was over, all he wanted to do was go to sleep so he could start another day with them tomorrow.

Chapter Twelve

Observant residents may have noticed there's no longer a camper parked behind Sutton's Place Brewery & Tavern, but rest assured Stonefield's favorite cowboy has not ridden off into the sunset! Lane Thompson let curious customers know the camper will be back tomorrow and Irish will be back behind the bar.

—*Stonefield Gazette* Facebook Page

Watching the sun rise from the ocean shore in the middle of May might have been one of the most beautiful sights Irish had ever seen, but it definitely wasn't warm.

And while it was peaceful, he wouldn't say it was quiet, thanks to the furnaces kicking on and off up and down the row of campers. He personally wouldn't call it cold, but it was definitely chilly enough so he was thankful he'd bought a lot of wood from the campground store. He started a fire in the old truck rim the campground used as a fire ring and once it got going, put the metal cooking rack over the top so he could perk some coffee. It would be easier to make it in the camper, but he didn't want to wake Mallory and the boys, and he'd been making coffee this way for more years than he cared to count.

He sat in the chair, watching the waves roll onto the sand as the day slowly brightened, and tried to wrap his head around how he'd ended up in this place. He was sitting at the edge of the ocean, drinking his coffee, while a beautiful woman and two kids slept in his camper.

He wasn't sure he had a name for what he was feeling right now. There was no urge to get up and do something—to find work that would keep his hands busy and fill the hours. There was no tension in his body. And other than wishing Mallory was sitting in the chair next to him, he couldn't think of a single thing he'd rather be doing right now.

Contentment, he thought. He was a man who, in this moment, was content.

It was temporary, of course. He couldn't sit in this chair forever. And the beautiful woman and the two kids asleep in his camper weren't his. But he'd take this feeling while he could get it.

He was straining a second cup of strong, scalding hot coffee into his cup when he saw a little face appear in the camper window. A few seconds later, a littler face popped up next to him. Irish put his finger to his lips and they both grinned.

As quietly as possible, he opened the camper door. He had light-blocking curtains in the bedroom and the door was closed, so Mallory was probably still sleeping. He gestured for the boys to put their shoes and hoodies on and grabbed a few things from the fridge. Then he ushered them outside.

"I bet your mom would like to sleep in on her vacation day," he whispered, and they both nodded.

The pajamas they had on didn't look warm, even with sweatshirts over them, so he pulled two wool blankets from his tent and wrapped one around each boy before they settled in the chairs.

He was surprised when they seemed content to sit quietly, staring at the fire. They were usually on the move, and not quiet about whatever they were doing, but they were clearly still sleepy.

As much as she needed the rest, Irish knew Mallory would enjoy seeing Jack and Eli like this. With a sigh, he pulled his cell phone out of his pocket and flipped it open. It took him a minute to remember how to access the camera—he'd only used it once before, to send a photo to a livestock agent.

He managed to take a picture of Jack and Eli finally, catching the boys wrapped in blankets, staring sleepily at the campfire in the foreground. Mallory would like it, he thought. And he'd gotten it just in time because Eli started shrugging off his blanket.

"I have to pee," the boy said in a very loud whisper.

Of course he did. Irish knew the quiet time was almost over, and them going into the camper would be the end of Mallory's sleep-in. "Who's up for a quiet walk to the bathhouse?"

He managed to get them to the bathroom without too much chaos, but it was obvious they were fully awake now and the time for sitting quietly in chairs was over. But maybe he could extend it a little by making it a game. Having little experience with kids and barely having a childhood of his own, he panicked for a moment, but once the boys were done in the bathhouse, he crouched down so he could talk to them.

"I think it's time for a secret mission," he said in a quiet voice. "Like spies."

They both nodded, and Eli whispered, "I want to be a spy."

"Our mission is to explore this beach and collect shells without anybody knowing we're here. We have to be stealthy or the enemy will catch us."

"We can be stealthy," Jack promised, and Eli nodded solemnly. "What does *stealthy* mean?"

Irish had to choke off a bark of laughter with a stifled cough. "It means sneaky and very quiet."

"Who's the enemy?" Eli whispered.

"All the grown-ups sleeping in the campers. If we wake them up, they'll catch us finding shells and our mission will be over."

Much to his surprise, the mission lasted over an hour. It was a long time for the boys to be quiet, but they moved around the beach in their pajamas—sometimes in a low, crouching run that they'd probably seen in a movie. Sometimes they'd put their fingers to their lips, reminding each other to be quiet, and they did the funniest victory dances when they found shells. They had quite a collection going when an older couple emerged from a camper farther up the row and the game came to an end.

"Mom's still sleeping," Jack whispered when they'd gathered back at the firepit to admire the shells.

"I think she'll wake up soon, so let's start breakfast." When both boys took a step toward the camper, he shook his head and pointed to the fire, which had burned down to glowing red logs. "Nothing beats breakfast over an open fire."

As quietly as possible, Irish gathered the things he'd taken out of the camper earlier and then pulled a few items—including his trusty cast-iron pan—from the storage compartment. He was pretty sure the boys didn't have a lot of experience with campfires, but under his *very* watchful eye and with strict instructions, they got the bacon frying. Once the grease started popping and snapping, he moved them to the other side of the ring and cracked a bunch of eggs into a bowl for Eli to beat with a fork, while he showed Jack how to toast bread on the fire rack.

Once the bacon was done and transferred to a paper-towel-lined plate, he had the boys take it to the picnic table and cover it with another paper towel while he poured off most of the grease into the fire. After the flare-up died down, he had Eli pour the eggs into the pan while Jack buttered toast. He was showing them how to gently fold the eggs repeatedly so they wouldn't burn when the back of his neck prickled, and he turned to see Mallory watching them through the window.

She looked soft and sleepy, and her lips were curved into a smile as she watched the boys making their breakfast. Then her gaze met his and her eyes crinkled as her smile widened. His heart ached in his chest at the sweet sight of her, and he couldn't help it.

He smiled back.

Wrapped in a soft wool blanket that smelled so much like Irish it felt like being wrapped in his arms, Mallory sat on the picnic table bench and listened to her sons talking over each other as they ate and shared tales of the morning's adventures of secret missions and cooking on a fire.

She was in so much trouble.

Every time her gaze met Irish's—and he was sitting across from her, so it was a lot—she fell a little deeper into that trouble.

When she'd opened her eyes that morning, she'd been as well rested as she could remember being in years—maybe even since Jack was born. The fresh ocean air and the Irish-scented sheets had lulled her into a deep sleep, and she'd woken to silence.

For a few minutes, she'd assumed Jack and Eli were still asleep, which would have been odd, but could be contributed to a day at the beach. Then she'd heard noises and the low murmur of voices outside, plus she'd smelled bacon, so she'd very reluctantly gotten out of bed. After a quick stop in the bathroom, she'd gone to the window and looked outside to see the view that had shoved her right off the edge of that trouble cliff.

Irish, Jack and Eli, all crouched next to a cast-iron pan, with their heads close together as Jack stirred the eggs. It was an image that she already knew was going to live in her mind and heart forever.

And that was *before* Irish had smiled at her.

He had *really* smiled. Not a slight curving of the lips, easy to miss with the beard, but a full smile that crinkled his eyes, showed the gleam of his teeth and made the now-familiar ache of wanting him flare up into a need that made it hard to breathe. Knowing on some deep, subconscious level he trusted her to see what he was truly feeling blew the lid off an emotional box she wasn't sure could be sealed again.

As soon as they were finished eating, the boys were on the beach. They knew they couldn't go in the water without an adult, but they could scour the sand and they had found a friend in a little girl four campers down.

Mallory was content to stay wrapped in Irish's blanket, sipping extremely strong coffee, and watching them play.

"Oh, I have something to show you." Irish pulled out his cell phone and flipped it open, an act which made her smile even as he scowled at the buttons. "I took a picture. Where…? Here, maybe you can find it."

She took the phone he held out to her and figured out how to navigate to his pictures. Then she frowned at him. "Is this a dead cow?"

"Oh, shi— Shoot. That was for a livestock agent who said I had to text it to him, and I ended up having to get one of the young kids to send it from my phone. I don't know how to delete pictures off that thing, but that's not the one I was trying to show you. Sorry." He gave her a sheepish look. "It'll be the other one."

"The other one? You only have two pictures on your phone?"

"Yeah. I don't know how to use the thing, really. People call me and I hit the green button. When I'm done talking, I hit the red button. Other than that, I've never cared enough to learn to do other things with it."

"Do you want me to delete the cow photo for you?" When he nodded, she laughed and deleted the photo, which automatically brought the next one up on the screen.

She stopped laughing as tears sprang to her eyes. It was one of the sweetest pictures of her boys together that she'd ever seen. Cuddling in blankets, with their sleepy, dreamy eyes looking at the fire. And taken by a man for whom using a cell phone was a struggle, but who had gone to the effort of capturing the moment for her. The same man who'd wrapped her sons in the blankets so they wouldn't be cold and then played a spy game with them so Mallory could get more blessed sleep.

How could she be falling so hard for a man she'd only known for six weeks?

And why did she let herself fall so hard for a man who wasn't staying?

Even in the early afternoon, the water was cold enough so the boys would run in for a few minutes, but then they walked on the beach, exploring and finding treasures to bring back to the picnic table. She had every intention of only letting them keep a few things, but they had quite a pile going.

Then she heard Jack yell, "Don't touch that, dummy!"

"Jack." Irish didn't raise his voice, but her son's head whipped around. "Are you calling your brother names again?"

"Sorry, Irish."

It was weird to hear somebody else correcting the boys, especially in a stern, deep voice. She'd been a single mother for most of their lives, so they'd had their grandpa, but he wasn't great at discipline and most of the time they were getting in trouble, it was their mother or grandmother speaking to them.

"It's not me you owe the apology to," Irish said.

"Sorry, Eli." Jack's gaze flicked to Mallory, and then back to his brother. "That's broken glass, not a shell. You have to be careful on the beach."

The boys moved on, and she was about to, but Irish didn't move. He was watching her, his body stiff. "What's wrong?"

"I shouldn't have spoken to Jack like that. I'm sorry."

"You didn't do anything wrong. He's not supposed to call Eli names."

"Maybe it wasn't *wrong* to speak to him, but it bothered you. I could see it on your face." He pressed his lips together for a moment, his eyes sad. "I grew up rough. You know that, but I wouldn't… I'm not like that."

She put her hand on his arm, leaning in so he could see her face. "I know you're not. I am *not* afraid of you being around my boys. If you won't believe me saying it to you, then think about my family. If for a single second any of us thought you might raise a hand to Jack or Eli, you would have been down the road a long time ago. That's not what's happening here. Do you believe me?"

His eyes warmed. "I do."

"If you saw something on my face when you spoke to Jack, it was probably just because it was a new—and very deep voice—speaking to them. Lane and Case are kind of the fun uncles, so it mostly falls to my mom and I to be the stern ones. It surprised me—that's all. I promise."

"I'm accustomed to being in charge, and it's probably also just in my nature. I'll try to rein it in, but I can't make any promises." He tipped her chin up with his fingertips so she was looking into his eyes. "But what I *can* promise you is that if I say something to the boys about what they're doing, it's never going to come from a place of disrespect for you. You're an incredible mother, Mallory."

Sadness cast a shadow over his expression for a fleeting moment, and she wondered if he was thinking about his own mother. Had she been incredible? Or did he regret that maybe she hadn't been? He never talked about his family, and she'd glimpsed enough of those shadows to make her reluctant to ask.

"If I overstep with Jack and Eli," he continued,

"just tell me. Give me a look. Something. But we're not out on the range here, so it's not my place."

Those words—*it's not my place*—made her ache in a way she didn't want to think about while he was looking at her so intently.

"I like the way you are with them," she said. "Let's walk and talk about something else."

"Okay, but you do the talking. I want to know more about you."

"You know me pretty intimately," she said, giving him a cheeky grin.

"That I do. But I mean, like…what got you to where you are now."

"You mean Jack and Eli's dad?" She supposed it was natural to be curious after spending so much time with the boys, and when he nodded, she realized she wanted him to know.

"I had it all once," she said, grabbing her water bottle as they passed by the picnic table. "A husband I loved and two amazing children. We had a cute little house on the other side of town, and Jeff installed a white picket fence just because the idea of having one made me laugh. We didn't have a dog yet because I wanted to wait until the boys were both potty-trained before I had to housebreak a puppy, but I was living the dream."

"Did he cheat?" Irish asked, with extra growl in his voice.

"No. I think that would have been easier, actually." When his face darkened, she blinked back the tears that were threatening to gather. "Whatever you're thinking, no. He was a sweet, gentle guy."

"It's okay if you don't want to talk about this," he said, clearly having seen the sheen of unshed tears.

"No, it's okay. It's behind me, to the extent that's possible, and also I don't want you thinking ill of him. Not that it matters, I guess, but he is Jack and Eli's father."

"It's hard not to think ill of a man who'd up and leave those boys," he said, and she felt a swell of emotion at the simmering anger in his voice. He might not think so, but she suspected he'd be an amazing father someday.

But the thought of him having babies with some other woman made her stomach ache, so she turned her focus back to the conversation at hand.

"When Eli was about nine months old, Jeff went snowmobiling with some of the guys and broke his leg pretty badly. Two-surgeries kind of badly." She took a sip of her water, hoping it would help loosen the knot gathering in her throat. She stopped and leaned against a boulder to watch her sons start building sandcastles, and Irish stood next to her. "They gave him some heavy-duty painkillers."

She watched understanding dawn in Irish's eyes and he covered her hand with his, his thumb gently stroking her skin. "I'm sorry."

"The boys don't remember it, thankfully, but it

got pretty bad, pretty fast. And when they refused to give him more prescriptions, it got worse." She knew she didn't have to lay it all out for Irish. He knew. "He was in jail for the second time when I divorced him. I had to in order to protect myself and the boys legally and financially, and he understood that. He actually made changing the boys' last name along with mine part of the divorce, because my parents are so well-liked in Stonefield he thought being Suttons would help people forget their dad and the trouble his addiction got him into."

"That had to be hard for all of you."

She nodded. "It was very hard for a while. He had made a mess of things while my attention was on two babies, and I didn't even work at the time. The only reason I didn't lose the house to foreclosure is Daphne—you've met Case's aunt at the tavern—bought it. She paid cash, just like that, so at least I could start fresh without that weighing me down, and then she flipped it once the dust settled and gave me a cut of the profit, even though she didn't have to. The boys and I moved in with my parents and I started working at the thrift shop and...here we are."

"And where is he?"

"I don't know, and I haven't known for years. I could probably search for him on the internet, but what good would that do, other than keeping me stuck in the past?" Mallory sighed. "I figure if he hasn't hit bottom and gotten the help he needs, I can't have him around my kids. If he does get that help and he's really okay, then someday he might reach out and want to see them."

He laced his fingers through hers and gave a comforting squeeze. "Would you let him?"

"If he's really committed to recovery, yes," she said, nodding. "He was a good man and a good husband. A great, loving dad. It wasn't his fault, and I tried as long as I could, but..."

"Mallory," he said, letting go of her hand so he could cup her cheek. "You did what you had to do. I wouldn't even have to hear the story to know that you did everything you could for him and for your sons because that's who you are."

She sniffed back tears. "I'm trying so hard not to cry."

"If you need to cry, then cry. But I like it better when you laugh," he said, giving her another real smile. "What can I do to make you laugh?"

"You look pretty funny with marshmallow in your beard."

He shuddered. "Please don't make me eat another s'more."

She laughed, dispelling the lingering sadness, and they started walking again. "Should I tell the boys they're building their sandcastles too close to the waterline? One good wave is going to wipe them out."

"Isn't that part of the fun of sandcastles? You build them and fix them up and then a wave crashes over them and the sand is smooth again, like they never existed."

Like Irish, she thought. They were building a sandcastle together, molding and shaping a relationship that was making her feel things she hadn't thought she'd feel again. She'd even dug a moat around them, keeping everybody else out.

But eventually a wave was going to sweep him out of her life.

Chapter Thirteen

There's a new survey on the town's website and they're looking for your opinions on the parking situation in Stonefield. Trucks and SUVs just keep getting bigger and after a recent debate over whether an SUV should have been given a parking ticket for not being within the lines when a tape measure proved that SUV was longer than every on-street parking spot, there's been a motion to consider repainting the lines. But remember, bigger spots mean fewer of them!

—*Stonefield Gazette* Facebook Page

The next morning, they had to check out of the campground by eleven, so Irish handled making the breakfast and cleaning up so Mallory could have as much time on the beach with her boys as she could.

He was a little sorry he hadn't gotten to see her in a bathing suit, but she'd put one toe in the water yesterday and declared it was far too cold for her. But she'd had a good weekend and he'd liked the way she'd wave to him from her chair under the awning while he splashed with Jack and Eli. And he'd really liked sitting with her in front of the campfire again after the boys fell asleep, talking until the campground was still and quiet in the darkness.

But all good things had to come to an end, so eventually they had to start packing up. He'd already stashed the outside stuff in the storage compartments, and now the boys were helping him secure everything inside while Mallory arranged stuff in the cab of the truck. She wasn't sure if the boys would sleep or not, but she had pillows for them, along with snacks and drinks.

"I wish we didn't have to go home," Eli said, and Irish agreed with the sentiment, but he felt a pang at the word *home*.

Technically, they were *in* Irish's home. He was thankful for the camper because it was the first residence he'd ever owned, but it being on wheels didn't really lend itself to any sense of permanence. Home meant something to Jack and the rest of them—it was the foundation of their lives, and the one place they could always rely on. For Irish, the camper represented not having to take a ranch job he didn't really want or rent some apartment that stuck him in some town with no other prospects just so he had a roof over his head.

He knew at some point, he'd probably settle somewhere. But for now, this was it.

"Maybe we can come here again," Eli said, and the hope and low-key excitement in his voice twisted Irish's gut and he didn't have the heart to tell the kid this was a one-time shot—that he was going to move on at some point in the near future. This was what Mallory had been worried about, he thought.

"Maybe," he said, not able to make a promise he couldn't keep, but equally unable to totally dash the kid's hopes.

"This was the best weekend of my *whole* life," Jack said.

Irish ran his hand over the boy's spiky hair, emotion making his throat tight. "Mine too, Jack."

He opened the drawer where he'd stowed his wallet and phone during the quick swim he'd taken after breakfast and transferred them to his pockets, thinking about the day they'd checked in. He'd known the boys would be in a hurry to get in the water, so he hadn't taken the time to put them away and Mallory had gone inside to wash the sunscreen off her hands.

She had to have seen it. But he knew it hadn't been moved because he could visualize the way the phone and his keys had been rested on the wallet. It would have taken her mere seconds to peek at his license and see the name he'd been given at birth.

He didn't care if she knew. It wasn't some dark secret he was keeping. He just hated the name and preferred not to use it, and it meant a lot to him that given that temptation, she'd chosen to respect his privacy.

Mallory poked her head through the open camper door, looking around. "How's it going in here?"

"We put the bucket of shells in the cabinet so they're safe," Eli told her, as if that was the most important thing. "But Irish said if we forget them and his camper stinks, he's going to hide egg salad in our room as payback."

Mallory wrinkled her nose. "I guess he's serious, then. And you should ask Grandma about the time we went to the ocean and shells got left in her car during a heat wave."

"Did she put egg salad in your room?" Eli asked.

"No, she didn't. Moms don't like to use punishments that make *more* work for themselves," she said, and then she gave Irish a pointed look that made him smile.

It felt good to smile, and the expression was beginning to feel more natural. And he really liked the way Mallory's face lit up when he did it.

When it came time to hook the camper back to the truck, Irish had the boys sit in the cab. While he grew a little more accustomed to their energy every day, he liked that energy restrained by seat belts while he was backing his truck up.

They were checked out and ready to leave with three minutes to spare. Considering how the campsite had looked that morning, he considered it something of a miracle.

"We'll be back in time for the taproom to open," she said as he slowly pulled the camper out of the site, and he couldn't tell if she was happy about that or not.

"Back to the real world," he said, and deep down, he was *not* happy about it. He would happily spend the rest of his days in this spot with Mallory, Jack and Eli. He'd even live on s'mores if he had to.

Before he made the turn onto the main road, he couldn't help pausing and looking out at the campground and the ocean beyond one more time. He hadn't been lying when he'd agreed with Jack that this had been the best weekend of his life.

A Friday afternoon through a Sunday morning, he thought. Such a short time to have changed him so profoundly, but it had happened. Something had shifted inside of him, and he hadn't had the time or space to process it all, but he didn't feel like the same man leaving as he had arriving.

"Did you forget something?" Mallory asked, and he realized he'd just been sitting there with his foot on the brake.

"Just looking at the ocean one more time," he

said, because he didn't have the courage to tell her the truth.

He was memorizing the place where he'd finally admitted to himself he was falling in love with her.

They made good time going home, which wouldn't have made Mallory happy, except the window between reconnecting the camper to the carriage house and opening the taproom got a little longer. Just long enough so she could leave her sons to recap their entire weekend for the grandmother, while she went out to help Irish "clean his camper" without them underfoot.

"So that's what the kids are calling it now?" Irish asked when she told him she'd dumped them on her mom. "'Cleaning the camper'?"

He locked the door and had half her clothes off before she even finished explaining they didn't have much time. She laughed as he buried his face in her neck, fumbling with her bra clasp.

"I said we didn't have much time, but we have a few minutes."

"And I intend to use all of it." He nipped at her earlobe as her bra finally released and he could cup her breasts. "I've been dying to touch you."

"Remember what you said about the apple pie being better if you've spent some time craving it?"

"Sweetheart, this weekend was like having a freshly baked apple pie all hot and fragrant, straight from the oven, set in front of me and being told I can't have a bite."

Then he nipped at her jaw—a gentle bite—before taking her hand and leading her up the two steps to his bedroom. She had no doubt in a proper house, he would have swept her off her feet and carried her, but in the space they had to work with here, she'd probably just end up concussed.

As soon as she hit the mattress, he stripped the rest of her clothes off before tossing his on the floor with them. She ran her hands over his chest and his shoulders as he lowered himself over her, and her heart somersaulted when he smiled at her. She was definitely getting used to that.

He kissed her thoroughly, starting with her mouth and working his way down. He loved to run his tongue over her taut nipples, making her shiver, but he didn't linger before kissing his way down her stomach.

Mallory couldn't take it—didn't want to wait another second—and she buried her hands in his hair to stop him. "I need you inside me, Irish. Now."

"Yes, ma'am," he said in that low, husky voice that made her pulse race.

After reaching into his drawer for a condom, he slid it on and nudged her knees farther apart so he could settle between them. She lifted her hips as he pushed into her, raking her fingers over his back. There was no finesse—he was as hungry for this as she was—and he rocked his hips, thrusting harder and deeper with each stroke.

When he reached between them, his thumb making circles over her clit, the orgasm came fast and hard. She bit her knuckle to keep from crying out his name as he moved faster. He groaned as he climaxed, pounding against her and she wrapped her legs around his hips, urging him on.

When he collapsed on top of her, she wrapped her arms around him and held him tight.

His breathless chuckle surprised her, and she wished she could see his face. "What's so funny?"

"I guess the problem with craving apple pie too much is that you just wolf it down instead of taking the time to savor it."

"Sometimes you just need to get that apple pie down," she said, kissing his shoulder. "You can savor a second helping later."

"Mmm." Very reluctantly, he pushed off her and disposed of the condom before fixing their nest of pillows and pulling her into his arms.

Far too soon, the pleasure fog lifted and the list of things she needed to get done and *should* be doing instead of lying in bed with Irish started creeping back into her mind. What she wouldn't give to be able to just fall asleep in his arms without a care in the world. She wanted to wake up next to him.

"It's John."

Frowning, she propped herself up on her elbow

so she could see his face and rested her free hand on his chest. "John?"

"My name. John Daniel Irish." He paused, and she could feel his heart hammering under her palm. "Junior."

"I wasn't expecting that."

"For me to tell you my name?"

"Well, that either. But mostly I didn't expect your name to be John. I thought it would be something… I don't know…something embarrassing. Something people would make fun of you for."

"Not many people make fun of me."

Since her hand was currently resting on the broad wall of his chest and had recently explored the rest of his hard body, she could see why not. And despite the distraction that body offered, her mind stayed focused on the fact his name was John. *John.* It was a perfectly good name, but it didn't fit him at all, and it would feel weird to use it. "So did you tell me that so I'll call you John now?"

"No."

Even though it was the answer she was hoping for, there was so much tension in that single word—and his heart was still beating so fast under her hand—that she knew there was a lot more to the story than him just not liking his first name.

"I told you because I wanted you to know," he continued, his voice tight. "But the only time I use it is for legal documents. I'm named for a man who was too full of bitterness and hate to be a father, and I refuse to honor him by using it. I thought about changing it once—legally, I mean—but by then I was used to being just Irish and didn't see the point in spending the money and going through the hassle of paperwork."

"Just Irish suits you better, anyway." His face softened, his body relaxing slightly under her hand, and she realized just how vulnerable he'd felt sharing something that most people wouldn't think twice about.

And because he'd been so open, she couldn't leave him just yet. Resting her head on her shoulder, she nestled against him and told herself that, no matter what, she couldn't nod off. It wasn't easy with him stroking her hair, though, because it made her want to close her eyes.

Five minutes later her phone chimed, signaling it was time for her to get out of Irish's bed and put her clothes back on. Especially once she found her phone under her pants on the floor and read the text message from her mother.

They're starting to wonder what's taking you so long. Just letting you know.

"I have to go," she told him as she pulled on her clothes. "I feel bad that I didn't actually clean any of your camper, though."

"Don't feel bad." He was propped against the pillows, his hands behind his head as he watched her get dressed. "It'll give you an excuse to come back tomorrow."

She laughed as she did a final check to make sure nothing was on backward or inside out, and then she paused to look at him. One kiss, she told herself. She could climb onto the bed, give him one more kiss, and then back out without her clothes coming off.

"Moooooom!"

Irish chuckled at her expression. "Go. I'll see you in the taproom."

Someday, she told herself as she left the camper and walked across the drive to where Eli was waiting to complain about Jack being bossy. Someday she was going to fall asleep in Irish's arms, and his face was going to be the first thing she saw in the morning.

Chapter Fourteen

Get your dancing shoes on, Stonefield! This Thursday, Sutton's Place Brewery & Tavern will be hosting the dance party of the year! Molly Cyrs is in charge of the playlist for the event, so expect lots of upbeat music, but with a cowboy in residence, you might hear a few country songs.

—*Stonefield Gazette* Facebook Page

Irish knew when they got back on Sunday that Evie had concocted a plan for a dance party in the taproom. Thursdays were their quietest night, so it made sense to do it then, but he'd heard Mallory arguing that three days' notice wasn't enough.

The argument had been that there was almost no planning involved. They would move the tables to the outside walls, leaving the center of the floor open for dancing, and Molly was going to hook her laptop to speakers and DJ the event. That's all there was to it, Evie said, and people who danced got hot and sweaty, and hot and sweaty people bought drinks.

Evie wasn't the one moving the tables, Irish thought as he and Lane set the last one in place. They still had to move all the stools and the clock was ticking toward opening hour, but Mallory walked through the door with two glasses of lemonade, and he decided it was a good time to take a break.

"Thanks," Lane said when he took a glass from her. "Though we have lemonade here, you know."

"I know," she said. "But that's store-bought lemonade. This is Mom's, and you know it's better."

When she turned to hand Irish his glass, their gazes locked and he thought maybe she didn't give a damn about store-bought-versus-homemade lemonade. Maybe she just used it as an excuse to see him for a few minutes.

She didn't stay because her mother and Molly were going over the playlist for the night and there was a hot debate raging about whether or not the Chicken Dance should be exclusive to weddings. And Gwen wasn't helping because she loathed the Chicken Dance and kept arguing for its total abolishment.

"Pretty sure Case mentioned how much he was looking forward to doing the Chicken Dance at their wedding," Lane said, and Mallory laughed.

"You're not helping."

When she went back to the house, humming the Chicken Dance song, Irish watched her leave, slowly sipping the lemonade. This all felt so *normal* to him right now. He could imagine the rest of their lives going just this way—quiet days with work and the boys and her family, and then nights together, just the two of them.

Then he cleared his throat and downed the rest of the lemonade so he could get back to work.

What was wrong with him that he was even considering the possibility of a life with Mallory? He had nothing to offer a woman like her—a woman surrounded by loving family in a beautiful home and raising two really great kids.

The closest he'd come to having a decent family was the guys in the bunkhouse, and everything he owned fit in the cabinets of a camper. He'd never seen himself getting married or having kids, so he'd simply never acquired more than what he needed to do his job.

And he wouldn't know the first thing about being a parent. While he remembered a few tender moments with his mother, life had been too hard for the Irish family to leave time for making good memories together. He didn't remember a time life wasn't about working and scraping together food to put on the table, and the harder it got, the meaner his father got. Jack and Eli had a childhood so different from his own, Irish had a hard time picturing himself in it.

That wasn't totally true, he admitted to himself. He *could* picture himself watching Jack and Eli grow up. He just knew Mallory couldn't picture it. He wasn't the kind of guy a woman like her chose to spend the rest of her life with.

The knowledge he had to hit the road—and soon—settled like a lead weight in the pit of his stomach.

He went to set his empty glass on the counter, to bring in later, and Lane was there, looking serious. "I've been wanting to talk to you about something."

In Irish's experience, those words led to long, complicated conversations. They weren't as bad as a terse *We need to talk*, but they were close. "Let's hear it."

"Would you be interested in buying into Sutton's Place?"

Irish leaned forward, resting his elbows on the bar. Lane certainly didn't beat around the bush. "Buying into the brewery? You mean, like an investor?"

People wanting to borrow money was familiar to Irish, but not only getting paid back, but possibly making a profit would be a new twist.

"Not just as an investor, but as a brewer." Lane sighed. "Case is a good guy and he's taken up a lot of slack for me while I put my energy into getting this place up and running but it's been months with no end in sight. The fact is, he and I own a business together and it's well past time I start pulling my weight again. You being here when I haven't been able to has made a difference."

"I didn't know you were thinking along those lines," he said in a noncommittal way.

"We need more people, already. And Evie's going to leave." Judging by the pain in his friend's expression, Irish knew Lane wasn't only anticipating the taproom losing a bartender when she left. It was going to hurt on a personal level.

"Has she said she's leaving?" Irish was pretty sure Mallory would have told him if her sister had said anything to her.

"No, but I can see it coming. I know her and she's already got one foot out the door." Lane's jaw clenched, but then he gave a sharp shake of his head, as if refocusing himself. "Molly's great but she doesn't technically work here and the day may come when helping out for fun isn't fun for her anymore. Besides the brewing, you're really good behind the bar. If you stay, we can expand our hours and the days we're open without the risk of hiring full-time help or putting more on Ellen and Mallory. That's more income for everybody."

Irish was doing his best to keep thoughts of Mallory out of his head, since this was first and foremost a business discussion, but it wasn't easy. "How do you see it working, exactly? Are you talking about selling me part of your stake?"

Lane held up a hand to indicate he didn't really know. "If you're interested, we'd obviously have to take it to Ellen, and to a professional. Me selling you half of my half leaves a lot of this on Ellen's plate. Ideally, I think the entire thing would be restructured so she retains some ownership—it's Sutton's Place, after all—but gets an influx of cash from you that can pay down her debt a little faster, plus a proper lease agreement between the business and her, as the property owner."

"That wasn't built in already?"

Lane shook his head. "It was one of the ways David saw to trim the operating budget—by not paying rent to himself. But losing David changed a lot of things. This was his dream and while Ellen went along for the ride, she didn't necessarily want to drive if you know what I mean."

"I understand that."

"We only pulled this off because we all pitched in. Gwen and Evie came home, and Case helped and… Let's just say without free labor and a whole lot of volunteer hours, it wouldn't have happened. It's truly a family business. And it's thriving and we're in this for the long haul. As far as Ellen, Gwen, Mal and Evie go, this is their home. Not only because it was David's dream, but because it's *literally* their home.

They're always going to be the heart and soul of this business. And I want them to be here as much as they want, but I don't want them to *have* to be." Lane paused, taking a swig of beer. "Ellen and Mallory have the thrift store and the boys. Jack and Eli have been really good for the last year about not getting as much time with their mom as usual, but it's not sustainable and it's not fair to them. They have activities and Jack's talking about sports and, to be honest, they kept their mom and grandma pretty busy *before* the brewery."

"And Gwen writes," Irish said, getting Lane's point. "She's here a lot in the evenings, though."

"Yeah, but she and Case are looking to give Jack and Eli a cousin or two in the near future." He paused again, his jaw clenching and relaxing. "And it's never a good idea to depend on Evie sticking around."

Irish's cell phone vibrated and he pulled it out of his pocket, assuming it must be Mallory because she and Lane were the only people who called him anymore, and it couldn't be Lane. But when he flipped it open, he frowned.

406.

Somebody was calling him from Montana.

That was weird. He put the phone back in his pocket, assuming if it was important, they'd call back. Or leave a message, in which case it might be a while before they got a response because he'd have to remember how to listen to his voice mail.

"I know it's a lot," Lane said. "But I hope you'll give it some thought."

If it was only up to him, Irish knew he'd jump at the chance to buy into the brewery. Good beer. Good people. He even liked talking to the customers.

But there was Mallory to consider. All of the decisions she'd made for herself regarding their relationship had been based on the understanding he was going to leave town. He couldn't change the rules on her midgame.

"I'll definitely give it some thought," he told Lane. "And I'll let you know."

It was pretty much all he thought about while they got ready to open the doors for Sutton's Place Brewery & Tavern's first ever dance party. And to make everything more complicated, the Montana number had tried again and there was a damn good job waiting for him if he went back west—a job that he wouldn't hesitate to take if coming to this place hadn't changed him. He'd asked for a week or two to think about it, but the idea of leaving Mallory and boys in two weeks made his chest ache so badly he rubbed the spot with the palm of his hand.

It all hinged on Mallory. If she didn't see a future with him, he would leave. There was no way in hell he could work with Lane and see her every day on a platonic level. That horse wasn't going back in the barn.

All night he talked with customers. When he

wasn't chatting with them, he was thinking about Mallory. About his future and whether or not it would include her. And how he was supposed to muster up the courage to talk to her about it.

He also watched the customers dance. But more importantly, he watched Mallory watching them dance. Every time she stepped out of the kitchen, she'd linger, swaying slightly to the music and smiling. Then she'd disappear again. They were so busy, Gwen and Case had even shown up to help, and Mallory still didn't get a break.

It wasn't right. She should have a turn on the dance floor, but Irish had never danced a day in his life.

No, that technically wasn't true. He had a very hazy memory of dancing with his mother in their shabby kitchen while she sang a Patsy Cline song, until his father heard them laughing and reminded them they had nothing to be joyful about. He never saw his mother dance in the kitchen again, and Irish certainly hadn't.

But for Mallory, he'd figure it out.

"The kitchen's closed for five minutes," he told Evie as he passed through the opening between the end of the bar and the kitchen wall.

She looked confused. "But—"

"Closed."

Mallory was about to pick up a bus pan full of dirty glasses when he turned the corner into the tiny kitchen. Her eyes widened, and then she smiled as she straightened, which made his already racing pulse kick it up another notch.

For a few seconds, he was tempted to dance with her right here, where nobody could see him making a fool of himself. But he couldn't dance with her in the kitchen. He didn't want any memories of his mother—or even worse, his father—casting a shadow. And Mallory deserved better than a stolen dance surrounded by dirty dishes.

He held out his hand. "Come dance with me."

She laughed, but took his hand. "Why?"

"Because you've been watching everybody else dance all night and it's your turn."

He was aware that Evie's eyes widened as he led Mallory out to the edge of where the dancing was happening, and that half the people in the room were watching them. It made him a little queasy, actually, but he turned to Mallory and stepped closer to her.

"I've never done this before," he admitted in such a low voice that she probably read the words on his lips rather than hearing him.

Smiling, she closed the gap between them and put his hands at her waist before resting hers on his shoulders. Then her body swayed, and it felt natural for his to just sway along with her. After a moment, he managed to slide his feet a little and she moved with him, but he was still aware that what they were doing didn't look a lot like what other couples were doing.

He dipped his head so he could talk close to her ear. "I think I should be moving my feet more."

"This is perfect."

"And I'm sorry everybody's watching us. I wanted to dance with you and didn't think about how it would get everybody talking."

"We watch each other constantly. I disappear with you at random times. We went away for a weekend together. I'm pretty sure people were already talking."

She had a point, and thankfully she didn't sound upset about it. "Friends do those things, too."

"You didn't take Evie or Gwen away for a weekend at the ocean, though, did you?"

He snorted. "I don't think I'd mess with Lane or Case. They look lean enough, but they're deceptively strong. I think they could take me."

She tilted her head to look at up at him. "You think Lane would fight you over Evie?"

Damn. He'd walked right into that one, and he still didn't know if Evie had told her sisters what had happened. "I don't know. A guy's not supposed to take his buddy's ex-wife to the ocean for the weekend, so he might just on principle."

That seemed to satisfy her and she rested her cheek against his chest. He felt self-conscious with everybody watching them—though they were doing a poor job of trying to pretend they weren't—so he closed his eyes.

It was easier that way. There was just Mallory in his arms, moving slowly with each other to a beautiful love song.

Mallory barely heard the music change to something far too upbeat to slow dance to. There was a pile of dirty glasses to run through the autoclave. Somebody probably wanted nachos. The popcorn machine was running low. Everybody in the taproom was watching them.

She didn't care.

They slow danced until somebody who was very enthusiastically dancing to the actual beat bumped into her and the spell was broken.

She smiled up at Irish. "Thank you for the dance."

There was a moment—a moment that should have been a kiss but couldn't be—when he just looked at her, and then he tipped his hat. "The pleasure was all mine, ma'am."

A woman nearby sighed, and Mallory rolled her eyes as she made her way to Molly, who was monitoring the laptop, while Irish went back to the bar.

"Way to make a statement," Molly said once Mallory was close enough to talk to without being overheard.

"It wasn't a statement. He felt bad I was stuck in the kitchen all night and didn't get to dance."

"Say whatever you want, but we're the ones who had to crank the air conditioning up because the heat radiating off the two of you was going to make everybody's beer warm." Molly heaved a dramatic sigh. "Nobody likes warm beer, Mal."

"I just came to say hi, but I'm going back to my kitchen now."

Her best friend's laughter followed her as she made her way around the outskirts of the dance floor, watching for rogue elbows. Irish was at the taps, filling glasses, but he gave her a scorching look as she walked past.

That look was going to have to carry her for a while, because she didn't get a chance to be alone with him for the rest of the night. By the time they could shoo everybody out, they were exhausted and the place was a mess.

"You guys go," Evie told Lane, Case and Irish. "Moving the tables back can wait until tomorrow, and the three of us will clean up anything that can't wait and turn everything off."

"Go a lot faster with six of us," Case pointed out before Irish could say the same thing.

"We've got it," Evie insisted, and there was something about the way she said it that had Mallory concerned.

"You guys go ahead," she said. "We're going to take our time and probably gossip while we work."

As soon as the door closed behind the men, the

words burst out of Evie as if she'd been holding them in and couldn't do it a second longer. "I'm leaving."

"Already?" Gwen snapped. "You *just* sent the guys home because you said we were going to clean up."

"No, I mean leaving town." She looked frustrated and that was never a good sign. "I came back to Stonefield and did my part, but now it's time for me to get back to my life."

An instant rejection of that plan blindsided Mallory—the three of them were a team, dammit—but she didn't want to respond in haste, so she looked at Gwen. She was the oldest, and while she and Evie didn't always communicate well, they'd been doing so much better this year. But judging by the expression on Gwen's face, she didn't know what to say, either.

"Molly's behind the bar half the time, anyway, and I'm pretty sure we can afford to pay her at this point. And when she can't be there, Lane can cover it. You don't need me here anymore."

"You handle all the social media," Mallory reminded her.

"Gwen's been doing some of it, and Molly loves Instagram. And I'll still keep an eye on everything. If I think of something that needs doing, I'll have you take pictures to send to me. I can do it all remotely."

Mallory could tell by the decisiveness in her tone that Evie had given this a lot of thought and she'd have an answer to anything they threw at her. "Where are you going?"

"I don't know yet. But it's time for me to go."

"You don't have to," Gwen said quietly. "I thought I'd leave, too, but I didn't."

"Well, unlike you, *I* didn't fall in love while I was here," Evie snapped, her tone uncharacteristically harsh. Then tears welled in her eyes and she shook her head.

Concern chased away any worries Mallory had about the brewery. Something was very wrong with her sister. "What's going on, Evie? This isn't just wanderlust. Something's wrong."

"I can't live like this—with Lane a part of my everyday life, but also not *really* a part of *my* life. It hurts too much."

"You still love him," Gwen said, and it definitely wasn't a question.

"He hasn't had a real long-term relationship since your divorce, and neither have you," Mallory said. "Maybe your story isn't finished."

The smile Evie gave her was the saddest Mallory had ever seen. "There's no happy ending for Lane and me, Mal."

It didn't happen often, but Mallory was totally at a loss as to how to help make this better for her sister. It wasn't possible for Evie to avoid Lane because if Lane wasn't cutting trees with Case, he was in the brewing cellar or in the taproom. Their dad had woven his and Lane's lives together in such a way it wasn't possible for Evie to be here and not be tangled up in it.

And they couldn't keep Lane away. Not only did he have a right to be on the property and in their lives on a daily basis, but they weren't going to maintain a very successful brewery without a brewer. And even if they were misguided enough to think they could learn how to do it themselves, they certainly didn't have the money to buy him out.

"Don't, Mal." Evie smiled. "I can see your brain working, trying to smooth this over, but just let me go."

"I don't want to let you go. I've gotten used to this—to the three of us being here together—and I like it."

"I like it, too," Gwen said. "It's been good for all of us."

"But it's getting *less* good for me, Gwen. I love seeing you and Case happy together. And Mallory and Irish."

"Irish isn't staying," Mallory pointed out, trying to hide how much saying the words aloud crushed her. They were closing in on that one-month mark, and since he hadn't said anything about staying longer—hadn't so much as mentioned what he might do when it was too cold for his camper—she wasn't letting herself hope he'd changed his mind.

"Yeah, we'll see about that," Evie said. "Nothing makes me happier than seeing my sisters happy, but it also amplifies the fact I'm not. And there's no chance I'll ever be as long as I'm seeing Lane every day. I can't stay here."

"When are you planning to go?" Gwen asked.

Evie took a deep breath. "Tomorrow, after the boys get home from school so I can say goodbye, but before the taproom opens."

"Tomorrow?" they both echoed at the same time.

"I want to get on the road and be going the opposite way of all the people traveling to the coast for Memorial Day."

"It's a long weekend," Gwen said, "and Mom's planning to close for Sunday so it's a two-day weekend for the family. Surely you can stay for that."

"No, I can't, because I keep telling myself to leave and then just staying for the next thing. There's always a next thing. I've been gathering up my stuff for a few days, trying to make up my mind, but now it's time to go, and I can't take a long, drawn-out goodbye with you all trying to get me to stay. This dance is my last hurrah, and I'm out of here tomorrow."

Mallory recognized her little sister's expression and nothing they said was going to change her mind. She could only hope Evie would change her mind on her own, which could happen. Gwen had left, and then turned around and come home, but Case had gone after her. Lane wouldn't go after Evie.

Maybe this was the weird vibe she'd been feeling all night, she thought. Maybe her subconscious had known the situation between Evie and Lane was about to come to a head, but she'd been denying it. She'd thought at first it was Irish. There were times he'd looked a million miles away, lost in thought. And then he'd danced with her and everything had felt right again.

"I hope you won't stay gone too long," she told Evie, feeling the tears welling up.

"No tears," Evie yelled. "Seriously, I'm so sick of crying. Let's crank up the music and sing while we clean."

Chapter Fifteen

The online form to suggest a new name for High Street has been deactivated due to an abuse of the system. We're told there are many benign words that have alternative meanings in certain online communities, and doing a Google search will result in images being displayed. One of our selectmen, who prefers not to be named, said, "I wanted to bleach my eyeballs". Alternative name suggestions will now be accepted exclusively in person at the town hall.

—*Stonefield Gazette* Facebook Page

The energy was different without Evie in the house, Mallory thought as she let herself in after a hectic day at the thrift shop. It had been a week since her sister said goodbye and hit the road, and it had thrown every aspect of Mallory's life out of whack.

The boys missed her. Her mother missed her, as did her sisters. The work flow in the taproom *definitely* missed her. And Lane was almost unbearable. He would never admit he was missing Evie, but they could all see it.

The only constant was Irish. He'd been her rock for the last week, letting her vent and making her laugh and, when they could sneak a few minutes alone, making love to her.

"Mallory, is that you?"

She stopped short, since there shouldn't be anybody in the house. Her mom was still at the shop and the boys weren't home from school yet, so hearing a voice was startling enough so it took her a few seconds to recognize it was her sister's voice.

"What are you stealing now, Gwen?"

"Your *very lives*, Mallory!"

She laughed at the reference to Mrs. Eastman and found her sister at the bottom of the staircase. Her hands were empty, so she hadn't absconded with anything yet. "What are you after?"

"I needed to know how many steps it is from the doorway of Mom's bedroom to the front door."

"You and Case have stairs. And a bedroom and a front door."

"But I'm using *this* house as the model for the house in my book."

"Okay." Gwen had been writing for as long as Mallory could remember, so she was used to these sorts of things and rarely asked too many questions.

"That's all I needed, so I'll see you later."

Mallory shook her head as Gwen left, probably wanting to get back to her computer before she lost the thread of whatever scene she was writing, or had to come back and recount the steps because she'd forgotten.

A few minutes later, the most hectic part of her day began with the arrival of the kids. There was homework to oversee and chores to make them do, while starting to prep things for supper. Eating early on days the taproom was open had worked for a little while, but wasn't sustainable long-term. Now Mallory got things ready for her mom before she went out to the taproom. When Ellen had finished making dinner, she would text Mallory, who'd try to time her break to eat with her kids. It was harder now that Evie was gone, but Molly was usually around and never minded covering for them. She was a very social creature and pretending to work at Sutton's Place was her new favorite thing.

But this afternoon, her mom decided she wanted to mix things up a little. "You should work it out with Lane and Molly so Irish can take his break and come eat with us tonight."

Mallory was in the process of applying lip balm on the off chance she was able to sneak in some kissing with Irish, and she snapped the lid on it as a flush heated her cheeks. "I can try, but we're busy around dinnertime."

"I know, but I've barely seen him this week. It would be nice to see him at the table."

Mallory agreed, but the more time she and Irish spent together, the harder it was to act like "just friends" in front of other people.

"You know, he should just move into the house."

There was absolutely no way she heard her mother correctly. "What did you just say?"

"It makes sense."

"No, it doesn't." Mallory shook her head so emphatically a few strands of hair stuck to her freshly applied lip balm because it really, really didn't make sense.

Ellen gave a little laugh, waving away Mallory's reaction. "Of course it makes sense. I'm neither blind nor your uptight great-grandmother, Mallory. There's no reason he can't live here in the house, even if he hasn't gotten around to proposing yet."

Proposing. It took every bit of Mallory's self-discipline not to drop her face into her palm. Her mother thought at some point in the future, Irish was going to be her son-in-law and they'd all live as one big happy family in this house.

"Mom." She realized she had no idea what else to

say. She really didn't want to say anything at all, but she couldn't let her mom go on mentally planning a wedding. "Because you're *not* my uptight great-grandmother, you are surely aware that two people having sex does not mean those two people are getting married."

"You'd be a fool to let him go. That man would wrestle a bear bare-handed for you."

Even as she rolled her eyes at her mother's statement, Mallory had to acknowledge she wasn't wrong. But she was pretty sure that was Irish's nature. He'd wrestle a bear to protect *anybody* who wasn't as strong as he was.

And she *had* to let him go. He was going to move on, and she'd known that from the beginning. And when the house was dark and quiet, and she was alone in her own bed, she'd sometimes be able to admit to herself it was coming soon. If Irish didn't decide it was time to hit the road on his own, she was going to have to send him on his way before she got in any deeper. If that was even possible. "I think you're trying to fill a void from Evie leaving."

Ellen laughed, though the sound had a bit of an edge to it. "Trust me, honey, there isn't a person out there who can stand in for one of you girls. I miss Evie, but that has nothing to do with wanting Irish to stay. One, I like him and two, I think he's the one for you."

This was exactly what Mallory had been afraid

of. "Mom. We've known each other less than two months. Jeff and I knew each other since we were kids, but even once we started dating as adults, we took it slow. And if not for the accident, I think we'd still be married. Two months is like the blink of an eye."

"And sometimes that's enough. The day your father and I met, he told me he was going to marry me, and I told him I was free the next week."

"You and Dad did *not* get married a week after you met."

"No, we didn't. But we knew we were going to."

Mallory didn't want to continue this conversation. It was pointless because Irish wasn't going to move into the house. And she was flat out lying to her mother by denying a person could fall in love in less than two months, and she didn't like lying to her.

"I'm going to leave this kitchen and go pull some weeds before I have to go in the other kitchen," she said, walking away before her mother could object. "I need fresh air once in a while."

She was halfway across the yard, intending to take her frustrations out on some hapless vegetation, when she spotted Irish in the gazebo. He was sitting alone, staring out at the river, and it was unlike him to be so still during the day.

He looked up when he heard her footsteps on the wooden floor and smiled, patting the bench next to him.

"I needed some fresh air," she said, sitting down close enough so her knee could touch his. "But I don't want to interrupt. You look like you're thinking about something."

He nodded slowly. "I got a job offer the other day."

She laughed. "Is Case trying to steal you to work for the tree service? He said he was going to try."

"No, but if he had, that would have been three job offers, because I guess I technically got two."

He looked tense somehow, and he hadn't relaxed when she laughed, which was different for him. "What were the job offers?"

"Lane asked me about maybe buying into Sutton's Place and—"

"Wait, what?" Mallory pushed herself to her feet as a million thoughts flew into her head, none of them good. "No."

She knew she should say more than that, but she couldn't get everything running through her to come together into a coherent sentence.

After everything they'd gone through—all the stress and the work and the debt and fear—to bring her dad and Lane's dream to life, Lane wanted to bail? And why would he have discussed it with Irish before talking to her mother at least, if not to all of them?

She frowned, unable to believe the man had so little respect for them—for her mother. She couldn't even come up with words to express how angry she was.

Irish watched her, his expression unreadable, even to her. She could see that his jaw clenched, but other than that, not even his eyes gave away what he was thinking.

"The other job offer is back in Montana." He said the words without any inflection at all, and she stilled. "I've got an offer to run a ranch for an owner I've known a long time. He's a stand-up guy with a really good group of hands."

"Oh." She sat back down so abruptly, it was almost a collapse. That's why he was so unreadable, she thought. This was the distance leading up to him leaving. "Oh."

"It's a good offer. I'd be a fool to pass it up."

She couldn't stand to look at his stoic face because he was giving her nothing, so she shifted and stared at the river, just as he'd been doing. Maybe it helped.

This was it, then. She'd known he was leaving, and she'd been a fool to hope he would change his mind. She had nobody but herself to blame for falling in love with a man who was just passing through.

Her body felt numb, except for her chest. Her heart was breaking, and all she could do was look at the moving water while she struggled to shove the pain down—to get her emotions in check. She wasn't going to make a scene. That would make it harder on everyone, especially the boys. And she had too much self-respect for that.

She cleared her throat, praying the tremor making

her muscles feel weak wouldn't show in her voice. "Well, I guess every fun fling must come to an end."

He shifted his body slightly, but he said nothing and she didn't dare look at him to see what his expression was doing. It was going to take all of the self-control she could muster to walk away without breaking down. Looking at him wasn't going to help.

"You'll stay to introduce your beer, right?" she asked, forcing a brightness into her voice that she definitely didn't feel. "Mom wants to do it on the taproom's nine-month anniversary."

He nodded. "I wouldn't leave before Jack's birthday, anyway. I'll be here for that."

Jack's birthday.

Her sons were going to be devastated. There was no way around that because the relationship they'd formed with Irish had nothing to do with what he and their mother had been up to. They would be crushed when he left, and they were going to miss him for a long time.

She would miss him forever.

It was going to be so hard to keep going when all she wanted to do was crawl into her bed and cry for days. But she couldn't do that because her sons would need her to help them through saying goodbye. Her family needed her. The brewery needed her. Everybody always needed her.

Except Irish.

She'd survived her husband's drug addiction.

She'd survived letting go of him and the dream they'd been building together. She'd survived losing her father at a time when he was full of hope and determination to bring his dream to fruition.

She'd survive watching Irish drive away, too. But, good lord, it was going to hurt.

"Congratulations on the new job," she said. "I guess I'll see you later, in the taproom."

He reached for her hand as she turned away, but she couldn't. If he touched her, she would fall apart and she couldn't do that now. She couldn't do it here, so she kept walking.

Though he'd foolishly allowed the hope he was wrong to seep in, on some level, Irish had known this day would come. As Mallory had explained to Lane that night in the taproom's kitchen, everybody loved playing with a new toy. But eventually the newness wore off and it became just another toy in the toy box. Eventually the toy that had been so fun sifted down to the bottom, unwanted and un-played-with.

On a logical level, he knew the analogy didn't work. She wasn't tired of playing with him. She enjoyed that. The problem was that she *only* wanted to play with him. And he wanted more.

It was one thing to keep their relationship under the radar when it was temporary and he was camping right in her backyard. But if he stayed in town much longer, he was going to have to find a place to live that wasn't on wheels. He'd be Lane's and her mother's business partner. It all implied a certain level of permanence. And based on her expression when he'd told her about Lane's offer, she wanted no part of it.

He'd thought maybe the idea of him buying into Sutton's Place and sticking around would give her the sense of security she needed to let her family—including Jack and Eli—know how she felt about him.

Or how he'd *thought* she felt about him.

All he'd seen on her face when he told her about Lane's offer was a whole lot of being upset. And she hadn't even asked him to stay.

Well, I guess every fun fling must come to an end.

For three days, he'd suffered in this place, trying to hide his broken heart. Fortunately, he had a lifetime's worth of practice hiding his emotions. He rarely saw Mallory and, when he did, she greeted him with distance and brittle smiles. And Mrs. Sutton and Gwen had been taking Mallory's place in the taproom's kitchen, claiming she wanted time with the boys.

She was avoiding him, and it confused the hell out of him. If she was okay with him leaving—and he had to assume she was, based on her reaction to Lane offering him an avenue for staying—why was she acting like this?

He couldn't wrap his head around it, but he also

couldn't bring himself to ask her. It was painful enough without asking for a flat-out rejection.

Now he was stuck trying to pretend everything was okay because they were celebrating Jack's birthday and he wasn't going to ruin it for the boy. Mrs. Sutton, who'd cried real tears when informed he would be leaving, had told him they'd rather wait until after his birthday to tell the boys he was going. He was dreading that day, so he was happy to put it off.

They'd done the cake first, since Jack had requested an ice cream cake, and now they were on to opening presents. As much as he liked Jack, Irish was anxious for the party to wrap up. While the boys were oblivious, the adults were all aware he was leaving and no matter how hard they tried to hide it, he could feel their disappointment in him.

"This card says from 'Mom, Grandma and Irish.'" Jack giggled. "That's funny."

He saw Mallory turn to him, her brows knit in a questioning look, but he wasn't about to spoil the surprise by explaining before Jack got to see his gift. Mrs. Sutton adding his name to the card was unexpected, but he should have guessed she would. She was a thoughtful woman, even if he didn't feel like he'd done enough to merit the credit.

"The card is empty," Eli pointed out, as if Jack hadn't already noticed.

"The gift that goes with the card is in the shed," Mrs. Sutton said, and both boys took off running.

Jack nearly came undone when he got the shed doors open and saw the bicycle. Irish saw Mrs. Sutton talking quietly to Mallory, and he assumed she was telling her that she'd pulled the bike from the thrift store after a conversation with him. Irish had hidden the bike in a corner of the brewing cellar and spent the last several weeks cleaning up the frame and replacing the brakes and cables. He'd oiled the chain and checked the tires over, but they'd only needed air. He'd been afraid Mallory wouldn't approve, since she'd told her son no and was hoping to get him a bike for Christmas, but she was smiling. And there was definitely no anger in the happy look she gave him.

"Thank you," she mouthed.

It was the first smile she'd given him since the gazebo and it hit him like a blow to the chest.

After putting on his helmet and doing a couple of careful laps around the driveway, Jack set the bike on its kickstand and dropped his helmet in the grass as he hugged his mother and then his grandmother. Then the boy was running to him, and Irish was about to extend his hand, expecting a handshake, when Jack threw his arms around his waist.

"Thank you, Irish!"

He had just enough time to rest his hand on the top of Jack's head for a moment before he was off and running back to the bike. Irish watched him go, something that felt an awful lot like affection making the corners of his lips twitch ever so slightly.

It was more than affection, he admitted to himself. It was going to be almost as devastating to leave Jack and Eli as it would be to leave Mallory. And not just because they were so much a part of who their mother was, but for who they were. He liked them a lot. They liked him. Not being able to see how they turned out was going to be a big void in his life.

When the ache in his chest deepened and he could barely swallow past the lump of emotion in his throat, Irish faded into the background and then quietly disappeared into his camper. He couldn't pretend to be okay anymore today.

He had a few more days to get through because he'd promised Mrs. Sutton he'd be there to introduce his beer—the one he'd brewed for Mallory, though her mother didn't know that—and he wouldn't break it.

And then he was going to have to dig deep and find the strength to drive away, leaving everybody he ever loved behind.

Chapter Sixteen

Today we have a fun update from Sutton's Place Brewery & Tavern! Come Friday night, to celebrate nine months of business. There will be a new beer on tap and it was brewed by their very own cowboy. It'll be a limited special edition, so make sure to stop by and see what everybody's favorite bartender has cooked up!

—*Stonefield Gazette* Facebook Page

"This is amazing," Lane said, wiping the back of his hand across his mouth. "I still can't believe you pulled it off."

Irish knew it was amazing. He wouldn't have settled for anything less because, in his mind, the brew that Lane had just sampled for the first time was for Mallory. Nobody else knew that, but he did. And it was damn near perfect.

"There's gotta be a way I can make you stay," Lane continued. "I mean, you came up with this, Irish. You were born to brew beer."

When Irish had first broken the news to Lane that he was going to have to turn down his offer to buy into Sutton's Place, he'd obviously been disappointed, but he'd accepted the decision. But now that he knew what Irish was really capable of in the brewing cellar, that might change.

"I've mostly minded my own business because it keeps me out of the drama," Lane said, and Irish braced himself. Here it came. "You leaving here will be the biggest mistake you'll ever make in your life."

Irish arched an eyebrow at him. "I might have a passion for brewing, but that's a pretty big claim."

"Brewing?" Lane snorted. "I'm talking about you leaving Mallory."

Irish felt his face freeze as every muscle in his body tensed. He didn't want to talk about Mallory. He couldn't stop himself from thinking about her, but he wasn't the type to hang his emotional laundry on the line for all to see.

"I know you don't want to talk about it," Lane said easily. "But we've known each other a long time and we've become pretty good friends the last couple months, so if anybody's going to say it, it's gotta be me."

"It's not an easy thing."

"Leaving her or talking about it?"

Irish tilted his head. "Both."

"Then just listen. They talk about how you feel electricity between two people and there's sparking and tension and whatever. But when you two are together, you're both more…I don't know…peaceful. There's a quietness about you together. Not that there's no heat. I've seen the way you two look at each other, but it's like you and her together are the way it's supposed to be. That probably doesn't make any sense."

It did make sense, because that's exactly how Irish felt when he was with Mallory. Whole. But he couldn't say that because his throat was so tight with emotion, he was afraid he wouldn't get the words out. He nodded, though.

"You said you were passing through," Lane continued. "So Mallory was willing to take what happiness she could while you were here and then let you go, because that's Mal. She puts everybody else first. And you're going to leave because you don't think she wants you to stay."

Every instinct Irish had was telling him to nod and walk out of here. Just leave it at that. But he couldn't do it and eventually he couldn't stop himself from asking the question. "You think she wants me to stay?"

"I'm not going to answer that for you. You'll have to

man up and ask her yourself. But you could ask yourself if we'd even be having this conversation if I didn't think you were the man for Mallory, and whether or not I'd have her best interests at heart over yours."

"You didn't see her face," Irish said, the memory making the words harsh and his voice rough. "When I said you'd asked me to buy in and stick around… she wasn't happy to hear it."

Lane frowned, and then he took another sip of the brew in his hand. "Damn, this is good."

"You've got the recipe."

He shook his head. "Somehow I don't think I could get it just right."

Irish had poured enough of his heart into it that he hoped Lane was right about that, though he didn't say so.

"Tell me something," Lane said. "Did you make it absolutely clear that I asked you to join us because it would make life better for all of us, including Ellen, with a total restructuring? Or do you think there's a possibility that all she heard was that after everything her family has sacrificed since David died, I'm looking to bail?"

Irish frowned, trying to remember the conversation. "I know I didn't tell her you wanted to bail on the brewery."

"But is it possible her gut reaction was thinking I wanted out, and that her reaction was about me and not about you staying?"

"I don't know."

"Is it *possible*, though?"

Irish considered it, his pulse quickening as hope struggled to make itself felt. "I guess it's possible."

"I think you should find out for sure."

Irish wasn't sure he'd survive being rejected by Mallory. If he put himself out there and she told him to go…he couldn't even think about it. He'd gone through his life not expecting anything from people and not being disappointed. She'd made him *feel* and it was wonderful and terrifying and potentially devastating.

"I've known Mallory my whole life," Lane said. "We all grew up together and she's a good woman, Irish. She's the best of us, really. If you let her love you, she will love you with her whole heart, but you have to let her. And I know you love her."

Irish had to clear his throat twice before he could get any words out. "You know that, do you?"

Lane lifted the glass, swirling the liquid so the light passed through it. "I know you do. You should make sure she knows it, too."

The thought of putting himself out there—of baring his emotions like that—made Irish's stomach knot up, but the alternative to making himself vulnerable was leaving Mallory and her boys in his rearview mirror, and that hurt worse.

He just didn't know how to do it.

* * *

The last thing Mallory wanted to do was walk into the Sutton's Place taproom and celebrate the launch of Irish's special-edition brew. She was happy for him and his beer, but she wasn't in the mood to celebrate. Not when he'd be hooking that truck to his camper and driving away any day now.

But the text from her mom had made it clear that not only had Irish requested her presence, but that her mother wasn't taking no for an answer. It was a special occasion—nine months since they opened their doors—and Evie might be gone, but she wanted her other two daughters with her. Jack and Eli were tucked into bed, so she turned on the baby monitor she kept in the hallway so she could listen for them, hooking the receiver on her waistband, and then made her way across the driveway to the taproom.

"Mallory, you made it," her mom said as soon as she walked through the door, and it was an effort for Mallory not to roll her eyes.

"I didn't really have a choice. But I can only stay for a few minutes. You know I don't like leaving the boys alone in the house."

"Just a few minutes," her mom promised. "It was important to Irish that you be here."

"Did he say that?" She tried her best to keep her voice neutral because Ellen was very perceptive and Mallory didn't want her to know how desperately she hoped Irish was thinking of her. And she expected her mom to dodge the question or give a nonanswer because it was probably more about her matchmaking than what Irish actually wanted.

"Yes, he did say it," Ellen said in a smug voice. "Oh, they're going to talk."

By *they*, she meant Lane and Irish, Mallory saw as she focused her attention on the bar. She watched Lane first, but she was still angry with him. She hadn't confronted him about wanting out of the brewery yet. One disaster at a time, and her heart breaking had claimed priority, plus with Irish leaving, it was temporarily a moot point. But once the dust settled, she and Lane were going to have a long talk.

Then her gaze shifted to Irish because she couldn't help herself. It hurt to look at him. And when he glanced around and his gaze met hers, the ache flared into a pain that took her breath away. He looked as unhappy in that moment as she felt, and a low hum of anger ran through her.

He was choosing to leave—to go back to Montana because of a job offer. He didn't have any right to look so miserable.

"You do it," she heard Irish tell Lane. The crowd had quieted to hear what was going on, so she had no trouble making out Irish's words. His voice carried, especially since she was so accustomed to listening for it.

Lane shook his head. "It's your brew. You do it."

"It's your bar."

"Again, it's your brew. Introduce it."

As Mallory watched, Irish's jaw clenched. He inhaled deeply and held the breath for a few seconds before letting it out. She wanted to touch his face—to soothe away the anxiety furrowing his brow—but that wasn't her place. He wasn't hers to touch anymore.

Irish stepped up to the bar and poured a quarter of a glass from the tap that wasn't labeled, the liquid a slightly cloudy but intense citrus color. Then he took out his wallet and retrieved a folded piece of paper from it. Mallory assumed he'd written a speech, but then he said a few quiet words to Lane and handed the glass and the paper to him.

Then Irish turned to the crowd. "Most of you know Lane and I have talked about beer for many years, so when he gave me the opportunity to brew up something special for you, I couldn't pass it up."

Mallory was watching him so intently, she was startled when Lane touched her arm. She hadn't even realized he'd come her way.

He pressed the folded-up paper into her hand. "He said to have a sip or two before you read it."

Then he gave her a half smile she couldn't decipher the meaning of before he headed back to the bar.

Irish was still talking to the crowd, but she couldn't resist taking a long sip of the beer he'd been working on. Flavor exploded in her mouth, citrusy like Evie's, but stronger and sweeter. Then, as she swallowed, the spice kicked in and her eyes widened.

She didn't know a lot about beer, despite the work they'd put into Sutton's Place, but she could tell this was a complicated brew with a lot of depth, and that surprise bite layered into the sweetness was a delight.

She set the glass down on the edge of the bar and then backed away. Her fingers shook as she unfolded the paper he'd been carrying in his wallet. The lighting was dim and his handwriting was small and painstakingly neat, so she leaned against the wall under one of the recessed can lights to read it.

> Mallory,
> You're all the things your father saw in you and I know you think that's boring but, trust me, there's nothing boring about loving and taking care of your family and being a great mom. There are sides to a woman that are only going to be seen by a man who loves her with his whole soul, though. I brewed this beer for you and since Jack could learn how to write a haiku, I figured I could, too.
>
> Sweetness laced with fire.
> A smooth touch that burns the soul.
> Unforgettable.
> I see you. And I don't want to go.
>
> Irish

It wasn't until a tear fell onto the paper—thankfully not hitting the ink—that Mallory realized she was crying.

He saw her.

He loved her.

Irish might wrestle a bear for anybody who needed the help, but she knew in her heart she was the only person in the world he'd write a haiku for.

And he didn't want to leave her.

There was applause in the bar, and she realized he'd finished speaking and Lane was starting to pour samples of the brew. She didn't care about any of that.

She was looking for Irish.

Their eyes met and through the blur of her tears, she could feel the intensity of his gaze as he searched her face. She could see the question—and the anxiety over having put himself out there—in the lines of his face and the set of his shoulders, and she didn't have to think twice about her answer.

"I love you," she mouthed, and she watched his body relax suddenly, as if the air had been punched out of him.

And then he smiled—a wide, happy grin that showed off his teeth and made his eyes crinkle—and over the pounding of her heart, Mallory heard half the women in the room sigh.

Daphne actually fanned herself with a bar napkin. "Whew. I've said many times the man should smile, but maybe it's a good thing he's not going around unleashing that on us all the damn time. Especially since he's clearly taken, which we all knew before he did."

Laughter rippled through the crowd, but it faded quickly when Irish circled the end of the bar and walked toward Mallory without ever breaking eye contact with her. And when he reached her, he took off his hat and she knew he was going to kiss her right there in front of everybody. There was going to be no doubt how he felt.

And she couldn't wait.

Before he bent his head to hers, he used his thumb to wipe the tears from her cheeks. Then, using his hat to shield them from the view of everybody in the taproom, he lowered his lips to hers. The kiss was gentle for the space of a breath, and then his free arm wrapped around her waist and he pulled her close. He claimed her mouth with his, as he had so many times before, but it was different this time. He was claiming *her*, with their hearts fully involved.

Ignoring the cheers around them, Mallory savored the kiss and the delicious feeling that this man was hers. And she didn't have to let him go.

When the kiss ended, their gazes locked again and in his blue eyes she could see all of the emotions she was feeling reflected back at her.

After raising his hat in a salute to the customers, who had clearly enjoyed the show, he settled it back on his head. "Enjoy the beer. I'm taking a break."

Then he took her hand and led her through the

door, chuckling at the cheers and whistles that followed them out of the taproom. Once the door closed behind them, muting the sounds, he stopped and took a deep breath.

Then he took both of her hands in his and looked her in the eye. "I love you."

Three simple words, said in his rough voice shot with nerves, were all it took to set Mallory's world right again. "I love you, too, Irish."

"I'm sorry it took me so long to say it to you." He cleared his throat. "I thought you wanted me to go."

"I thought you *wanted* to go."

He shook his head. "I want to stay and make a life with you. A life with you and your boys and your family and the brewery."

"I want that, too. I want *you*." She smiled through her tears.

"Then I'm ready to settle down. Sell that camper. Make a home with you."

"The boys will be disappointed if you sell that camper. They liked camping with you. We all did."

"Oh, there's going to be camping because I liked camping with you, too, but I figure you and I should go find a camper together—one that has proper bunks for them to sleep in, all the way at the other end of the camper from our bed." Heat warmed her cheeks, and he smiled. "That camper brought me here, but it's time for a family camper."

"I like the sound of that."

"So do I."

He pulled her up against his body, letting go of her hands so he could wrap his arms around her. Their mouths met and as he kissed her, Mallory experienced all the feelings his kisses gave her, but without the question marks this time. No uncertainty. No threat of goodbye on the horizon. Their love was the forever kind of love, and she would be kissing this man for the rest of her life.

The kiss ended when they heard a faint squeal of excitement, and she looked over her shoulder to see two little faces in the upstairs bedroom window. Eli's head was actually bobbing as he jumped up and down, and she wasn't surprised when Irish lifted his hand and gestured for the boys to join them.

They hit the front porch running, in their pajamas with bare feet. Jack got to them first, but it was a close call. "If you're kissing Mom, does that mean you're staying?"

"How would you boys feel about me sticking around?"

Eli's eyes got big, but Mallory could see the hesitation in his expression. "For how long?"

Irish tilted his head. "I was thinking forever if you'll have me."

Mallory's breath caught in her throat when Eli threw himself against Irish, wrapping his arms around him. Even Jack, who was too quickly approaching the age where he wasn't as emotionally demonstrative, stepped forward enough so Irish could put one arm around his shoulders, while his other hand was pressed against Eli's back.

"We want you forever," Jack said quietly, and Eli's head nodded up and down so fast against Irish's stomach, Mallory smiled through her tears.

"So y'all are gonna marry me?" Irish asked, his eyes on Mallory's face.

"Yes!" both boys shouted in unison.

Mallory cupped his bearded cheek in her hand. "Yes."

"Are we all going to live in the camper with you?" Eli asked, pulling away from Irish, and they all laughed. "We have a *lot* of Lego toys."

But then Jack frowned slightly. "Do we have to buy a new house when you get married and leave Grandma? She'd be all alone, and Boomer would miss us, too."

"This is a pretty big house," Irish said, running his hands over Jack's hair. "If your grandma doesn't mind, I think I'll just live in it with you guys."

"She won't mind," Jack said immediately, his face brightening. "She says she likes having you around."

"We should go tell her," Eli said.

"You're not allowed in the taproom while we're open," she reminded them. "Especially in your pajamas, with no shoes on."

Irish chuckled. "Plus your grandma and your aunt Gwen have had their faces pressed to the window since we came outside, so I think they've already figured it out."

Mallory turned and saw that he wasn't exaggerating. Her mom and sister weren't even trying to be stealthy about their spying.

"We're getting married," Eli shouted to them in a decibel level that was impressive, even for him.

Gwen turned and said something over her shoulder, and cheers they could hear through the walls shook the taproom.

When Irish laughed, Mallory slid her arm around his waist and squeezed. "Welcome home, cowboy."

Epilogue

"Dance with me, wife."

Mallory laughed as Irish spun her into his arms. "There's no music, so I don't think it's time for the dances yet."

"I don't care." He pulled her close and swayed, so she swayed along with him until the sights and sounds of their wedding reception faded away.

They'd been married in the backyard, standing in the freshly painted and flower-draped gazebo with the river behind them and their friends and family in folding chairs on the lawn. Paul Cyrs, Molly's dad, had presided over the ceremony as justice of the peace, while Molly stood beside her and Lane at Irish's side.

The only cloud over the day had been Evie's absence, but she'd driven all the way to Arizona and didn't want them to put off getting married until she could make it home. She'd sent them Sutton's Place glasses with Bride and Groom etched in them, and Daphne had put herself in charge of carrying Evie around as her video chat plus-one. Evie hadn't missed a second of it, and was currently holding court at a corner table that was close enough to an outlet so Daphne could keep her phone charged.

As her husband spun her through the room, she caught sight of Jack and Eli, looking incredibly dapper in their white shirts with black bolo ties and black cowboy hats to match Irish's. The photo she'd taken of Irish helping them with the ties before the ceremony was already her phone's lock screen and she thought there might come a day when she could look at it without tears of joy and gratitude filling her eyes, but today wasn't that day.

"I hate to cut in," her mother said, "but it's almost time to cut the cake."

"You can cut in anytime, Mrs. Sutton." Irish took her hand and gave her a twirl.

"You're my son-in-law now," she said a little breathlessly, "so at some point you're going to have to stop calling me Mrs. Sutton, you know."

"I know…ma'am."

Ellen laughed and then reached up to cup his face in her hands, looking into his eyes for a long time. Then, as Mallory felt her insides go all warm and fuzzy, her mother tugged Irish's head *way* down so she could kiss his cheek. "Try *Mom* on for size when you're ready. Welcome to the family, Mr. Sutton."

Irish smiled, but his eyes glistened. "It's not official yet, but we're doing the paperwork."

It had been Mallory's idea, whispered in the dark one night. Having a wife and stepsons would mean having to use his full name—there would be years of school forms and more—and she knew how painful that was for him, so she'd asked him to share hers. He'd always be Irish, but he could share the Sutton name with people who loved him—the family who'd made him theirs—and with his wife and the boys he'd be a father to. He'd also see his name on the sign of the business he'd soon be a part owner of. She couldn't be sure, but she thought she'd felt moisture on his cheek when he'd kissed her.

He'd always be just Irish to them, but he was starting the process of changing his legal name to Irish Sutton before they hooked up the camper and went on their road trip honeymoon. It would be a short one because, even with Molly filling in, the taproom was a lot to handle, but she intended to enjoy every second of it. It would be the camper's last trip before they traded it in for a family-friendly model in the spring, and the boys would be staying home.

“Mom, it’s time for cake,” Eli yelled, and it was time for Mallory to share her husband with all the people crammed into the taproom.

They ate cake and drank beer—though her mother had insisted on one champagne toast—and every time somebody clinked silverware against their glass, they kissed. They kissed a *lot*, until Gwen threatened to replace the silverware and glasses with plastic and paper if they didn’t ration their PDA demands.

That had made Irish laugh, and Mallory’s eyes closed as she savored the rich baritone sound. The first time he’d laughed, it had surprised them both, but the walls he’d built around his emotions had crumbled pretty quickly.

After two hours of partying, Mallory was exhausted. Her groom was sitting in a proper chair—brought out from the dining room—so she kicked off her shoes and dropped sideways onto his lap. He brought his arm up to support her back as she smiled at him.

“You make a comfy resting spot,” she said.

“I’m afraid you’re going to slide right off my lap in this dress, though.” He brushed his hand over her satin-covered hip. It was a simple gown with thin straps and a deep V-neck, but no sequins or lace, and she'd fallen for it the second she saw it in the bridal store.

"I know you won't let me fall."

"Never."

They heard the tinny clanging of a metal spoon against a glass and Mallory saw Evie grinning at them from Daphne's phone. "Gwen can't take my spoon away."

Irish took his hat off and used it to hide their kiss from their guests, which was cheating, but they all cheered anyway. Then he set it on her head, careful not to mess up her hair, and grinned. "I love you, wife."

She was never going to get tired of hearing those words—of seeing that smile—and she raised her hand to his cheek so the lights glinted off the warm gold band on her finger. "I love you, too, husband."

Wrapped in his arms and surrounded by the people she loved most, Mallory looked around, soaking it all in. Her sons sneaking second slices of cake. The photo of her dad on the wall. Her mother beaming as she and Laura got a sneak peek at the pictures on the photographer's camera. Gwen and Evie's familiar bickering even though one of them was over two thousand miles away.

"I love this—all of this," she said, and then she tilted her head back to see his eyes. His hat slipped, and he caught it before it could fall and then settled it back on his head, where it belonged. "And I love you."

As many of you know, Stonefield's very own cowboy is officially off the market! Mallory Sutton and Irish were married yesterday in a private ceremony at home, and they followed it up with a not-so-private reception at Sutton's Place Brewery & Tavern! Make sure you congratulate the happy couple if you see them around town!

According to her mother, Evie Sutton attended all the way from Arizona, thanks to video chat. When Mallory tossed her bouquet, it bounced off hands like a hot potato, and Molly Cyrs almost caught it, but then it hit the phone screen and knocked Evie to the floor, so that was ruled a catch. Are wedding bells in Evie Sutton's future?

—*Stonefield Gazette* Facebook Page

* * * * *

COMING NEXT MONTH FROM

HARLEQUIN

SPECIAL EDITION

#2905 SUMMONING UP LOVE

Heart & Soul • by Synithia Williams

Vanessa Steele's retreated to her grandmother's beach house after she loses her job and her fiancé. When she finds out her grandmother has enlisted hunky Dion Livingston and his brothers to investigate suspicious paranormal activity, the intrepid reporter's skeptical of their motives. But her own investigation discovers that Dion's the real deal. And any supernatural energy? Pales compared to the electricity that erupts when the two of them are together...

#2906 A FORTUNE IN THE FAMILY

The Fortunes of Texas: The Wedding Gift • by Kathy Douglass

Contractor Josh Fortune is happy to be Kirby Harris's Mr. Fixit. Repairing the roof of Kirby's Perks is a cinch, but healing her heart is a trickier process. For three years the beautiful widow has been doing everything on her own, and she's afraid to let down her guard. She thinks Josh is too young, too carefree—and way too tempting for a mama who has to put her kids first...

#2907 SECOND-CHANCE SUMMER

Gallant Lake Stories • by Jo McNally

For golf pro Quinn Walker, Gallant Lake Resort's cheery yet determined manager, Julie Brown, is a thorn in his side. But the widowed single dad begrudgingly agrees to teach his sassy coworker the game he loves. As their lessons progress, Julie disarms Quinn in ways he can't explain...or ignore. A second chance at love is as rare as a hole in one. Can these rivals at work tee it up for love?

#2908 THE BOOKSHOP RESCUE

Furever Yours • by Rochelle Alers

Lucy Tucker never imagined how dramatically life would change once she started fostering Buttercup, a pregnant golden retriever. The biggest change? Growing a lot closer to Calum Ramsey. One romantic night later, and they're expecting a baby of their own! Stunned at first, steadfastly single Calum is now dutifully offering marriage. But Lucy wants the true-blue happy ending they both deserve.

#2909 A RANCH TO COME HOME TO

Forever, Texas • by Marie Ferrarella

Alan White Eagle hasn't returned to Forever since he left for college eight years ago. But when a drought threatens the town's existence, the irrigation engineer vows to help. An unlikely ally appears in the form of his childhood nemesis, Raegan. In fact, their attraction is challenging Alan's anti-romance workaholic facade. Will Alan's plan to save Forever's future end with a future with Raegan?

#2910 RELUCTANT ROOMMATES

Sierra's Web • by Tara Taylor Quinn

Living with a total stranger for twelve months is the only way Weston Thomas can claim possession of his Georgia family mansion. If not, the place goes to the dogs—seven rescue pups being looked after by Paige Martinson, his co-owner. But when chemistry deepens into more powerful emotions, is the accountant willing to bank on a future that was never in his long-term plans?

SPECIAL EXCERPT FROM

Mariella Jacob was one of the world's premier bridal designers. One viral PR disaster later, she's trying to get her torpedoed career back on track in small-town Magnolia, North Carolina. With a second-hand store and a new business venture helping her friends turn the Wildflower Inn into a wedding venue, Mariella is finally putting at least one mistake behind her. Until that mistake—in the glowering, handsome form of Alex Ralsten—moves to Magnolia too...

Read on for a sneak preview of Wedding Season, *the next book in* USA TODAY *bestselling author Michelle Major's Carolina Girls series!*

"You still don't belong here." Mariella crossed her arms over her chest, and Alex commanded himself not to notice her body, perfect as it was.

"That makes two of us, and yet here we are."

"I was here first," she muttered. He'd heard the argument before, but it didn't sway him.

"You're not running me off, Mariella. I needed a fresh start, and this is the place I've picked for my home."

"My plan was to leave the past behind me. You are a physical reminder of so many mistakes I've made."

"I can't say that upsets me too much," he lied. It didn't make sense, but he hated that he made her so uncomfortable. Hated even more that sometimes he'd purposely drive by

PHMMEXP0322

her shop to get a glimpse of her through the picture window. Talk about a glutton for punishment.

She let out a low growl. “You are an infuriating man. Stubborn and callous. I don’t even know if you have a heart.”

“Funny.” He kept his voice steady even as memories flooded him, making his head pound. “That’s the rationale Amber gave me for why she cheated with your fiancé. My lack of emotions pushed her into his arms. What was his excuse?”

She looked out at the street for nearly a minute, and Alex wondered if she was even going to answer. He followed her gaze to the park across the street, situated in the center of the town. There were kids at the playground and several families walking dogs on the path that circled the perimeter. Magnolia was the perfect place to raise a family.

If a person had the heart to be that kind of a man—the type who married the woman he loved and set out to be a good husband and father. Alex wasn’t cut out for a family, but he liked it in the small coastal town just the same.

“I was too committed to my job,” she said suddenly and so quietly he almost missed it.

“Ironic since it was your job that introduced him to Amber.”

“Yeah.” She made a face. “This is what I’m talking about, Alex. A past I don’t want to revisit.”

“Then stay away from me, Mariella,” he advised. “Because I’m not going anywhere.”

“Then maybe I will,” she said and walked away.

Don’t miss
Wedding Season *by Michelle Major,*
available May 2022 wherever
HQN books and ebooks are sold.

HQNBooks.com

PHMMEXP0322

HARLEQUIN